PUFFIN BOOKS
Editor: Kaye Webb
PS 292

DOCTOR DOLITTLE'S ZOO

After Dr Dolittle got back from his voyages and had given a wonderful surprise party and had told everybody who wanted to hear about his adventures, he settled down to look after all the animals who had become ill while he was away. Then he decided to tidy up his garden and turn it into a zoo, or to be more correct an Animal Town. He had lots of special places in it, like the Rat and Mouse Club, the Badgers' Tavern or the Squirrels' Hotel. And of course he had lots of Shops, Schools and Playgrounds, and, we are sorry to say, Police and Prisons: for animals can break the law as much as anyone else.

But it was a happy place and, like everything Dr Dolittle did, it turned out splendidly with lots of extra surprises no one expected, like discovering that the Beaver was eating gold from the land, just in time to help pay all the bills, or helping locate a missing will, and putting out a great fire. And even the prisoners enjoyed themselves, especially if, like the Prison Rat, they had a good audience to listen to their stories.

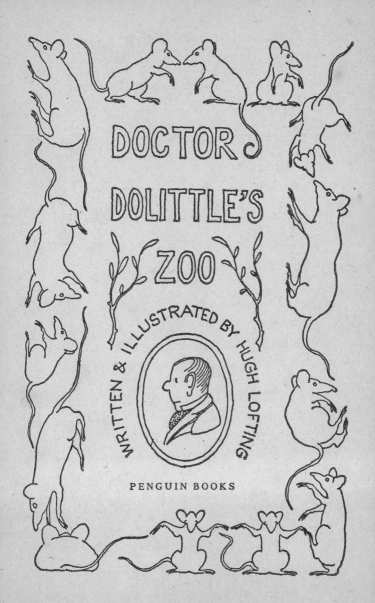

DOCTOR DOLITTLE'S ZOO

WRITTEN & ILLUSTRATED BY HUGH LOFTING

PENGUIN BOOKS

Penguin Books Ltd, Harmondsworth, Middlesex, England
Penguin Books Australia Ltd, Ringwood, Victoria, Australia

—

First published by Jonathan Cape 1926
Published in Puffin Books 1967
Reprinted 1967

—

Copyright © Hugh Lofting, 1926

—

Made and printed in Great Britain
by Hazell Watson & Viney Ltd,
Aylesbury, Bucks
Set in Linotype Pilgrim

CONTENTS

'POLYNESIA,' I said, leaning back in my chair and chewing the end of a quill pen, 'what should you say would be the best way to begin another book of Doctor Dolittle's memoirs?'

The old parrot, who was using the glass inkpot on my desk as a mirror, stopped admiring her reflection and glanced at me sharply.

'Another!' she exclaimed. 'Is there going to be *another* Dolittle book?'

'Why – er – yes,' I said. 'After all, we are writing the Doctor's life and we haven't nearly finished yet.'

'Oh, yes, I quite see that,' said Polynesia. 'I was only wondering who decides how many books there shall be.'

'Well, I suppose – in the end – the public does,' said I. 'But tell me now: how would you begin?'

'Thomas Stubbins, Esquire,' said she, screwing up her eyes, 'that's a very difficult question to answer. There is so much of interest in the life of John Dolittle that the problem is what to leave out, rather than what to put in. Already I see grey hairs showing at your temples, Tommy. If you try to write down everything the Doctor did, you'll be nearly my age before you've finished. Of course, you're not writing this book for the scientists exactly, though I confess I often think, since you are the only person so far – besides the Doctor – to talk animal languages at all well, that you ought to write something sort of – er – highbrow in

7

natural history. Usefully highbrow, I mean, of course. But that can be done later perhaps. As you said, we are still engaged on the story of the great man's life. ... How to begin? – Humph! Well, why not go on from where we all got back to Puddleby River inside the Giant Sea Snail, you remember? – after our journey under the ocean?'

'Yes,' I said, 'I thought of beginning there. But it was more *how* than *where* – I mean, the things to leave out and the things to put in; what parts to choose as the most interesting.'

'Ah!' said she. 'Yes, that's the problem. How often have I heard the Doctor himself say those very words as he was packing his little black bag to go on a voyage: "What to leave out and what to put in? That's the problem." I've seen him spend half an hour wondering over his razor – whether he should pack it or not. He said a broken bottle did just as well, once you had learned how to use it. You remember how he hated a lot of baggage. He usually decided to go without the razor. But Dab-Dab and I were so scared he'd cut himself with the broken glass we always secretly opened the bag later and slipped the razor in before starting. And as he never could remember which way he had decided the problem, it was all right.'

'Indeed,' said I. 'But you haven't answered my question yet.'

Polynesia pondered a moment.

'What are you calling the book?' she asked presently.

' "*Doctor Dolittle's Zoo,*" ' I said.

'Humph,' she murmured. 'Then I suppose you ought to get on to the zoo part as soon as possible. But first I think you had better put in a little about your own homecoming and your parents and all that. You *had* been away nearly three years, you know. Of course it's sort of sentimental. But some people like a little sentiment in their books. In fact, I knew an old lady once who simply loved books that made her weep. She used to – '

'Yes, yes,' I said hurriedly, seeing that the old parrot was drifting into another story, 'but let us keep to the point.'

'Well,' said she, 'I think this would be the best way : you read it all out aloud to me as you put it down; and if it starts to get tiresome you'll know, because you'll see me dropping off to sleep. You will have to keep it bright and lively though, for as I grow older I find it harder and harder to stay awake after lunch – and I've just had a big one. Have you got enough paper ? Yes. And the inkpot is full ? Yes. All right. Get along with it.'

So taking a new quill pen and sharpening the point very carefully, I began :

A MESSAGE FROM DAB-DAB

I T suddenly occurred to John Dolittle that in the excitement of getting back he had not said good-bye to the snail who had brought us through this long and perilous voyage and landed us safely on our home shores. He called to us to wait and ran down the beach again.

The farewell did not take long; and presently he left the great creature's side and rejoined us. Then for a few moments the whole party stood there watching, with our bundles in our hands, while the giant snail, half-hidden in the mists that writhed about his towering shell, got under way. Truly, he seemed to belong to this landscape – or seascape – for his long grey body looked like a part of the long grey sandbar on which he rested. With easy muscular motion, so fluid and smooth that you could not tell how he moved at all, his great hulk slid out into deeper water. And as he went forward he went down, and down, and down, till only the top of his shell's dome, a dim grey pink in the colourless sea, could be seen. Then, without sound or splash, he was gone.

We turned our faces toward the land, Puddleby and home.

'I wonder what supplies Dab-Dab has in the house,' said the Doctor, as we formed into single file and, following Jip, began to pick our way across the boggy marshland. 'I hope she has plenty to eat. I am thoroughly hungry.'

'So am I,' said Bumpo.

At that moment, out of the wet, misty air above our heads two handsome wild ducks curved fluttering down and came to a standstill at John Dolittle's feet.

'Dab-Dab asked us to tell you,' said they, 'that you're to hurry up and get home out of this rain. She's waiting for you.'

'Good gracious!' cried the Doctor. 'How did she know that we were coming?'

'We told her,' said the ducks. 'We were flying inland – there's a pretty bad storm over the Irish Sea, and it's headed this way – and we saw you landing out of the snail's shell. We dropped down at the house to let her know the news. We were awfully glad to see you back. And she asked would we return and bring you a message – she herself was busy airing the bed linen, it seems. She says you're to step in at the butcher's on the way home and bring along a pound of sausages. Also she's short of sugar, she says, and needs a few more candles, too.'

'Thank you,' said the Doctor. 'You are very kind. I will attend to these things. You didn't take long over getting there and back; it doesn't seem to me as though more than a minute had passed since we landed.'

'No, we're pretty good flyers,' said the ducks; 'nothing fancy, but steady.'

'Didn't you find the rain a great handicap?' asked the Doctor.

'No, the rain doesn't bother *us*,' said the ducks, 'though some of the land birds are very badly hampered by wet feathers. But, of course, for all, the going is a little slower in rain on account of the air being heavier.'

'I see,' said the Doctor. 'Well, now let us be getting along. Jip, you lead the way, will you, please? You can pick out the firm ground so much better than the rest of us.'

'Look here, you fellows,' said Polynesia, as the ducks prepared to take wing, 'don't be spreading the news of the Doctor's arrival too fast, will you? He's only just back from a long and tiresome journey. You know what happens when it gets known that he's home: all the birds and beasts of the countryside come around to the back door with coughs and colds and what not. And those who haven't anything wrong with them invent some ailment just to have an excuse to call. He needs to rest a bit before he starts doctoring.'

'No, we won't tell anyone,' said the ducks; 'not tonight, anyway, though a tremendous lot of wildfowl have been inquiring for him for ever so long wondering when he was going to get back. He has never been gone so long before, you see.'

'Humph!' muttered Polynesia, as the ducks, with a whir of feathers, disappeared again into the rainy mist above our

heads. 'I suppose John Dolittle has to give an account of his actions now to every snipe and sandpiper that ever met him. Poor man! How dare he be away so long! Well, such is fame, I suppose. But I'm glad I'm not a doctor myself. Oh, bless this rain! Let me get under your coat, Tommy. It's trickling down between my wings and ruining my disposition.'

If it had not been for Jip's good guidance we would have had a hard job to make our way to the town across the marshes. The light of the late afternoon was failing. And every once in a while the fog would come billowing in from the sea and blot out everything around us, so that you could see no farther than a foot before your nose. The chimes of the quarter-hours from Puddleby church tower were the only sounds or signs of civilization to reach us.

But Jip, with that wonderful nose of his, was a guide worth having in a place like this. The marsh was riddled and crossed in all directions by deep dykes, now filling up like rivers with the incoming tide. These could very easily cut off the unwary traveller and leave him stranded at the mercy of the rising waters. But in spite of continuous temptation to go off on the scent of water rats, Jip, like a good pilot, steered a safe course through all the dangers and kept us on fairly solid ground the whole way.

Finally we found he had brought us round to the long, high mound that bordered the Puddleby River. This we knew would lead us to the bridge. Presently we passed a hut or two, the outposts of the town. And occasionally in the swiftly flowing water on our left we would see through the lifting mists the grey, ghostly sails of a fishing boat coming home, like us, from the sea.

2

THE ADVENTURER'S RETURN

As we came nearer to the town and the lights about Kingsbridge twinkled at us through the grey mist Polynesia said:

'It would be wiser, Doctor, if you sent Tommy in to get the sausages and went round the town yourself. You'll never get home if the children and dogs start recognizing you. You know that.'

'Yes, I think you're right, Polynesia,' said the Doctor. 'We can turn off here to the north and get around on to the Oxenthorpe Road by Baldwin's Pool and the Mill Fields.'

So the rest of the party went off with the Doctor, while I went on into the town alone. I was a little sorry not to have been present at John Dolittle's homecoming, I must admit. But I had another thrill which partly made up for it. Swaggering across Kingsbridge, alone, I returned to my native town a conquering adventurer from foreign parts. Oh, my! Christopher Columbus just back from his discovery of the New World could not have felt prouder than I, Tommy Stubbins, the cobbler's son, did that night.

One of the little things that added to the thrill of it was that no one recognized me. I was like some enchanted person in the *Arabian Nights* who could see without being seen. I was three years older than when I had left, at an age when a boy shoots up and changes like a weed. As I swung along beneath the dim street lamps toward the butcher's in the High Street I knew the faces of more than half the folk who passed me by. And I chuckled to myself to think how surprised they'd be if I told them who I was and all the great things I had seen and done since last I trod these cobble-stones. Then in a flash I saw myself back again on the river wall, where I had so often sat with legs dangling over the water, watching the ships come and go, dreaming of the lands I had never seen.

In the Market Square, before a dimly lighted shop, I saw a figure which I would have known anywhere, seen from the back or the front. It was Matthew Mugg, the Cat's-meat-Man. Just out of mischief, to see if he, too, would be unable to recognize me, I went up to the shop front and stood, like him, looking in at the window. Presently he turned and looked at me. No. He didn't know me from Adam. Highly amused, I went on to the butcher's.

I asked for the sausages. They were weighed out, wrapped and handed to me. The butcher was an old acquaintance of mine, but beyond glancing at my old clothes (they were patched and mended and sadly out-grown) he showed no sign of curiosity or recognition. But when I came to pay for my purchases I found to my dismay that the only money I had in my pockets was two large Spanish silver pieces, souvenirs of our stormy visit to the Capa Blanca Islands. The butcher looked at them and shook his head.

'We only take English money here,' he said.

'I'm sorry,' I said apologetically, 'but that is all I have. Couldn't you exchange it for me? It is, as you see, good silver. One of these pieces should be worth a crown at least.'

'Maybe it is,' said the butcher. 'But I can't take it.'

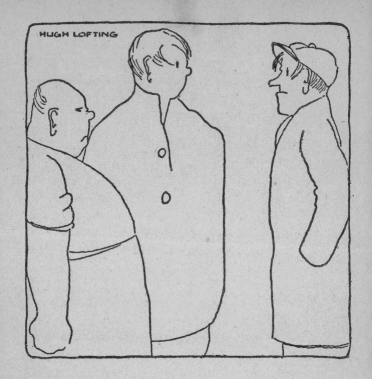

HUGH LOFTING

He seemed sort of suspicious and rather annoyed. While I was wondering what I should do I became aware that there was a third party in the shop interested in what was going on. I turned to look. It was Matthew Mugg. He had followed me.

This time his eye (the one that didn't squint) fixed me with a curious look of half-recognition. Suddenly he rushed at me and grabbed me by the hand.

'It's Tommy!' he squeaked. 'As I live it's Tommy Stubbins, grown so tall and handsome his own mother wouldn't know him, and as brown as a berry.'

Matthew was, of course, well known to the tradesmen of the town – especially to the butcher, from whom he bought the bones and odd pieces of meat for the dogs. He turned to the shopkeeper.

'Why, Alfred,' he cried, 'this is Tommy Stubbins, Jacob Stubbins's lad, back from furrin parts. No need to be worried about *his* credit, Alfred. He's shopping for the Doctor, I'll be bound. You brought the Doctor back with you?' he asked, peering at me anxiously. 'Don't tell me you come back alone?'

'No,' I said. 'The Doctor's here, safe and sound.'

'You're just in, eh?' said he. 'Tonight – eh? John Dolittle couldn't be in this town long without my knowing it.'

'Yes,' I said. 'He's on his way up to the house now. Asked me to do a little shopping for him. But all the money I have is foreign.'

I said this with the superior air of an experienced travel- ler, raising my eyebrows a little disdainfully at the obsti- nate butcher, whose stay-at-home mind couldn't be ex- pected to appreciate a real adventurer's difficulties.

'Oh, well, Alfred will let you have the sausages, I'm sure,' said Matthew.

'Why, yes, that's all right, Tommy,' said the butcher, smiling at my airs. 'Though we ain't exactly a money exchange, you know. But if you had said at first who you were, and who the sausages were for, I'd have charged them to the Doctor without a word – even though his credit hasn't always been of the best. Take the meat – and tell John Dolittle I'm glad he's back safe.'

'Thank you,' I said, with dignity.

Then, with my package beneath one arm and Matthew Mugg firmly grasping the other, I stepped forth into the street.

'You know, Tommy,' said Matthew, as we set off in the direction of the Oxenthorpe Road, 'all the years that John Dolittle's been returning from voyages he ain't never got home once without me to welcome him the first night he got in. Not that he ever tells me he's coming, mind you. No, indeed. As often as not, I fancy, he'd rather no one knew. But somehow or other I always finds out before he's been in the town an hour, and right away I'm up there to welcome him. And once I'm inside the house, he seems to get used to me and be glad I'm there. I suppose you've seen an awful lot of adventures and strange sights and things since I saw you last?'

'Yes, Matthew,' I said. 'We saw even more than I had thought or hoped we would. We have brought back notebooks by the barrow-load and a collection of wonderful herbs which were gathered by an Indian naturalist – frightfully valuable and important. And – what do you think, Matthew? – we came back inside the shell of a giant sea snail who crawled along the bottom of the ocean with us all the way from the other side of the Atlantic!'

'Oh, well,' said Matthew, 'there be no end to the strange things Doctor John Dolittle's seen and gone through. I've given up talking about his voyagings and queer doings. Down in the taproom of the Red Lion I used to tell about his travels – of an evening like, when folk enjoy a tale. But never no more. It's like this business of his speaking animal languages: people don't believe you; so what's the good?'

We were now some half-mile along the Oxenthorpe Road and within a short distance of the Doctor's house. It was quite dark. But in the hedges and the trees all about us I could hear birds fluttering and chattering. In spite of Polynesia's request, the news had already spread, in that mysterious way it does in the Animal Kingdom. The season was still cold and few more than the winter birds could be found in England now. But round about the famous Little House with the Big Garden they were gathered in thousands – sparrows, robins, blackbirds, crows, and starlings –

to welcome the great man back, prepared to sit up all night just to see him in the morning.

And it occurred to me, as I walked up the steps and opened the little gate at the top, that such was the great difference between this strange popularity and friendship that the Doctor enjoyed and that of ordinary human society: with some friends, if you were away three years, it would mean you'd find yourself forgotten when you returned. But with John Dolittle and his animal friends, the longer he was gone the greater the welcome and rejoicing when he came home again.

3

THE SURPRISE PARTY

As a matter of fact, I did not entirely miss witnessing the Doctor's homecoming. When Matthew and I entered at the kitchen door we found an air of mystery in the house. We had expected, of course, an enormous amount of noise – greetings, questions, and so forth. But there wasn't a soul even visible besides the Doctor himself – and Dab-Dab who promptly upbraided me for taking so long over getting the sausages.

'But where is Gub-Gub?' the Doctor was asking as we came in.

'How on earth should I know, Doctor?' said Dab-Dab. 'He'll turn up presently – and the rest of them, no doubt. Have you washed your hands for supper? Please don't leave it to the last moment. The food will be on the table in five minutes. I'll want you to help me, Tommy, with the sausages. By the way, Doctor, we're going to have supper in the dining-room.'

'In the dining-room!' cried John Dolittle. 'What on earth for? Why don't we use the kitchen as usual?'

'Not big enough,' grunted Dab-Dab.

I suspected from an odd look in the housekeeper's eye that there was some surprise in store. And, sure enough, when the dining-room door was opened, there it was. The whole crowd of them, Gub-Gub, Too-Too, Swizzle, Toby, and the white mouse, all in fancy dress. It was a surprise party given in the Doctor's honour.

The dining-room was a funny old stately chamber which the Doctor had closed up years and years ago – in fact, it had not been used since his sister Sarah had left him. But

HUGH LOFTING

tonight it was gaily decorated with coloured papers, ribbons, and evergreens. The animals were all in their old pantomime costumes, even the white mouse was wearing a tiny waistcoat and trousers in which he used to appear in the famous Dolittle Circus of bygone days.

Now, with the Doctor's appearance at the door, the noise which we had missed began in earnest. Barks, yelps and squeals of greeting broke forth. But there was very little disorderly behaviour, for apparently a regular programme of entertainment had been arranged. The meal was most elaborate, the table piled high with fruits and dainties of every kind. Between the courses each one of the animals who had stayed at home had some performance to give.

Gub-Gub recited one of his own food poems, entitled 'The Wilted Cauliflower'; Toby and Swizzle gave a boxing match (the stage was the middle of the table) with real boxing gloves tied on their front paws; and the white mouse showed us what he called 'The Punchbowl Circus'. This took place in a large glass bowl, and was the most thrilling thing of its kind I have ever seen. The white mouse was ringmaster, and he swaggered about on his hind legs with a tiny top hat on his head made of paper. In his troupe he had a lady bareback rider, a clown and a lion tamer. The rider was another mouse (using a cutlet frill for a ballet skirt), and she rode a squirrel for a horse – the fastest mount I ever saw. The lion tamer was still another mouse, and his lion was a large rat dressed up with strings on his head for a mane.

Taken all in all, the Punchbowl Circus was, I think, the greatest success of the evening. The white mouse had even, in a way, made himself up. With some heavy black grease paint, which Swizzle, the old clown dog of the circus, had lent him from his own private make-up box, he had waxed his whiskers together so that they looked exactly like the long, ferocious moustaches of a regular ringmaster. The lady bareback artist leapt through paper hoops, the mouse clown (also made up with a red-and-white face) threw somersaults, and the rat lion roared savagely.

'I don't know how on earth you all managed to get the show ready in time,' said the Doctor, tears of laughter running down his cheeks at the antics of the mouse clown. 'It's better than anything I ever had in my circus. And you only knew I was coming half an hour before I got here. How did you do it?'

'You'll soon see how it was done if you go upstairs, Doctor,' said Dab-Dab severely. 'It was Gub-Gub's idea. They turned the house inside out to get the costumes and

the ribbons, and they turned the garden upside down to get the evergreens. Tut! Such foolishness! And just when I needed every one of them to help me put the house in proper order against your coming.'

'Oh, well, never mind, Dab-Dab,' said the Doctor, still laughing. 'It was worth it. I never enjoyed anything so much in all my life. We can soon get the house straightened out. You have Stubbins and Bumpo and me to help you now, you know.'

'Yes, and I don't know where I'm going to put Bumpo to sleep, either,' said Dab-Dab. 'None of the beds we have will fit him.'

'Well, we'll manage,' said the Doctor. 'If the worst comes

to the worst we can put two mattresses together on the floor.'

'And now, Doctor,' said Gub-Gub, 'your part of the performance begins. We want to hear all about your travels since you left here.'

'Yes, yes,' they all cried. 'Begin at the beginning.'

'But, good gracious!' cried John Dolittle. 'I couldn't tell you our complete diary for three years in one evening!'

'Well, tell us some of it,' squeaked the white mouse, 'and keep the rest for to-morrow night.'

So, lighting his pipe, which, with the tobacco jar, Chee-Chee brought down off the mantelpiece, the Doctor began at the beginning – the tale of his travels. It was a wonderful scene – the long dining-room table packed all around with listening faces, animal and human. The Doctor's household had never, to my knowledge, been so complete before: Bumpo, Matthew Mugg, myself, Dab-Dab, Gub-Gub, Chee-Chee, Polynesia, Jip, Too-Too, Toby, Swizzle, and the white mouse. And then, just as he was about to begin, there came a thud at the window, and a voice said:

'Let me in. I want to listen, too.'

It was the old lame horse from the stable. He had heard the noise, and, realizing that the Doctor had arrived at last, had come across to join the party.

Greatly to Dab-Dab's annoyance the double French windows which opened on to the garden were unlatched and the old lame horse invited to join the party. The good housekeeper did insist, however, that I should brush his hoofs clean of mud before he was allowed in on to the carpets. It was surprising to see how naturally he took to such unusual surroundings. He passed through the room without upsetting anything and took up a place between the Doctor's chair and the sideboard. He said he wanted to be near the speaker, because his hearing wasn't what it used to be. John Dolittle was overjoyed to see him.

'I was on my way out to your stable to call on you,' he said, 'when supper was announced. You know how particular Dab-Dab is. Have you been getting your oats and barley regularly since I've been gone?'

'Yes, thank you,' said the old horse. 'Everything's been quite all right – lonely, of course, somewhat, without you and Jip – but all right otherwise.'

Once more the Doctor settled down to begin his story and once more he was interrupted by a tapping at the window.

'Oh, goodness! Who is it now?' wailed Gub-Gub.

I opened the window and three birds fluttered in – Cheapside, with his wife Becky, and the famous Speedy-the-Skimmer.

'Bless my soul!' chirped the Cockney sparrow, flying up on to the table. 'If anybody ever broke into this 'ouse 'e'd deserve all 'e could pinch. That's what *I* say. Me and Becky 'as been pokin' round the doors and windows for hours, lookin' for a way in. Might as well try to get into the Bank of Hengland after closin' time. Well, Doc, 'ere we are! The old firm! Glad to see you back. Me and the missis was just turnin' in up at St. Paul's when we 'eard the pigeons gossipin' below us. There was a rumour, they said, that you'd got back. So I says to Becky, I says, "Let's take a run down to Puddleby and see." "Right you are," says she. And down we come. Nobody can't never –'

'Oh, be quiet!' Too-Too broke in. 'The Doctor is about to tell us of his voyage. We don't want to listen to you all night.'

'All right, Cross-eyes, all right,' said Cheapside, picking up a crumb from the table and talking with his mouth full, 'keep your feathers on. 'Ow long 'ave *you* owned this

27

'ouse, anyway? Hey, Speedy, come over 'ere where it's warmer.'

The famous swallow, champion speed flyer of Europe, Africa, and America, modestly came forward to a warmer place under the branching candlesticks. He had returned to England a little earlier this year than usual, but the warm weather which had tempted him northward had given way to a cold snap. And now in the brighter light near the centre of the table we could plainly see that he was shivering.

'Glad to see you, Doctor,' said he quietly. 'Excuse us interrupting you like this. Please begin, won't you?'

4

THE NEW ZOO

So, far into the night, John Dolittle told his household the story of his voyage. Gub-Gub kept falling asleep and then waking up very angry with himself because he was afraid he had missed the best parts.

Somewhere around two o'clock in the morning, although he was not more than half done, the Doctor insisted that everybody go to bed and the rest of the adventures be put off until tomorrow night.

The following day was, I think, the busiest day I have ever seen the Doctor put in. Everybody and everything demanded his attention at once. First of all, of course, there were patients waiting at the surgery door : a squirrel with a broken claw, a rabbit who was losing his fur, a fox with a sore eye.

Then there was the garden, the Doctor's well-beloved garden. What a mess it was in, to be sure! Three years of weeds, three years of overgrowth, three years of neglect! He almost wept as he stepped out of the kitchen door and saw the desolation of it fully revealed in the bright morning sunlight. Luckily the country birds who had been waiting all night to greet him helped to take his mind off it for a while. It reminded me of the pictures of St Francis and the pigeons, as the starlings, crows, robins and blackbirds swarmed down about him in clouds as soon as he appeared.

Bumpo and I, realizing how deeply affected he was by the sad state of his garden, decided to put our shoulder to the wheel and see what we could do toward cleaning it up. Chee-Chee also volunteered to help, and so did a great

number of smaller animals like field mice, rats, badgers, and squirrels. And, despite their tiny size, it was astonishing to see how much they could do. For example, two families of moles (who are usually a great pest in a garden) dug up, after the Doctor had explained what he wanted, the entire herb bed next to the peach wall, and turned it over better than any professional gardener would have done. They sorted out the weeds from the herb roots and gathered them into neat piles, which Chee-Chee collected in his wheelbarrow. The squirrels were splendid as general clean-up men. They collected all the fallen twigs and leaves and other refuse which littered the gravel walks and carried them to the compost heap behind the potting shed. The badgers helped by burrowing down and pruning the roots of the apple trees underground.

Then, in the middle of the morning Too-Too, the accountant, wanted to go into money matters with the Doctor, so that Dab-Dab might see how much she had to keep house with. Fortunately, the Spanish silver we had brought back from the Capa Blancas (largely out of Bumpo's bet, which the Doctor didn't know anything about) looked, when changed into English pounds, as though it should keep us all comfortably for some months at least without worry. This was a great relief to Dab-Dab, though, as usual, she kept an anxious eye on any new schemes of the Doctor's, remembering from the past that the more money he had, the more extravagant he was likely to be.

It was a funny sight to see those wiseacres, Too-Too, Polynesia and Dab-Dab, putting their heads together over the Doctor's money affairs while his back was turned.

'But, look here,' Polynesia put in, 'the Doctor ought to make a lot of money out of all these new and precious herbs of Long Arrow's which he brought back.'

'Oh, hardly,' said I. 'You'll probably find he'll refuse to profit by them at all. In his eyes they are medicines for humanity's benefit: not things to sell.'

And then, in addition to all the other departments of his strange establishment which claimed the Doctor's attention that morning, there was the zoo. Matthew Mugg was on hand very early to go over it with him. Not very many of the old inmates were there now. Quite a number had been sent away before the Doctor left, because he felt that in his absence their care would be too ticklish a job for Matthew to manage alone. But there were a few who had begged very hard to remain, some of the more northerly animals like the Canadian wood-chucks and the minks.

'You know, Stubbins,' said the Doctor as we passed down between the clean, empty houses (Matthew had in our absence really kept the place in wonderful condition), 'I have a notion to change the whole system of my zoo.'

'How do you mean?' I asked.

'Well,' said he, 'so far I had kept it mostly for foreign exhibits – rather unusual animals – though, as you know, I always avoided the big hunting creatures. But now I think I'll give it over almost entirely to our native animals. There are a great many who want to live with me – many more than we can possibly manage in the house. You see, we have a big space here, over an acre, altogether. It used to be a sort of a bowling green hundreds of years ago, when an old castle stood where the house is now. It is walled in – private and secluded. Look at it. We could make this into a regular ideal Animal Town. Something quite new. You can help me with the planning of it. I thought I would have several clubs in it. The Rat and Mouse Club is one that I have been thinking of for a long time. Several rats and mice have asked me to start it. And, then, the Home for Cross-Bred Dogs is another. A tremendous lot of dogs – of no particular breed – call on me from time to time and ask if they can live with me. Jip will tell you all about it. I hate to turn them away, because I know many of them have no place to live – and people don't want them because they're not what is called thoroughbred. Silly idea. Myself, I've usually found that the mongrels had more character and sense than the prize winners. But there you are. What do you think of my idea?'

'I think it's just a marvellous idea, Doctor,' I cried. 'And it will certainly relieve poor old Dab-Dab of an awful lot of worry. She is always grumbling over the way the mice eat the pillow slips in the linen closet and use the fringes off the bath towels to make their nests with.'

'Yes,' said the Doctor, 'and we've never been able to find out who the culprits are. Each one, when I ask him, says *he* didn't do it. But the linen goes on disappearing, just the same. Of course, myself, I'm not particular if a pillow slip has an extra hole in it or not. And bath towels don't *have* to have fringes. But Dab-Dab's awfully pernickety. Her linen closet – gracious! – for her it is the same as the garden is for me: the most important thing! ... Well, now, Stubbins, supposing as soon as we get some of these poor old fruit trees into shape you plan out the new zoo for me. Get Polynesia to help you. She's full of ideas, as you know. Unfortunately, I've got my hands more than full already with the surgery and the writing

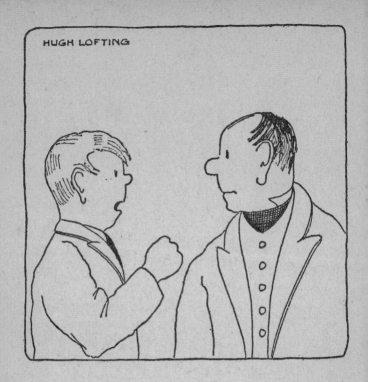

up of the notebooks we brought back (I'll want you to help me on that, too) – to say nothing of Long Arrow's collection. Otherwise I could work with you on the first lay-out of the zoo. But you and Polynesia can do it between you. By the way, consult the white mouse about the quarters for the Rat and Mouse Club, will you?'

Well, that was the beginning of the new Dolittle Zoo. It was, of course, a thing that interested me tremendously, and I felt very proud that the Doctor had entrusted such a large measure of the responsibility to me. But I had very little idea, at the outset, into what an enormous institution it was to grow. 'Animal Town' or 'Animal Clubland' is really what it should have been called, instead of a zoo.

But we had always called that part of the garden the zoo, and that name persisted.

But if it wasn't a regular zoo to the ordinary public's way of thinking, it was very certainly Doctor Dolittle's idea of one. In his opinion, a zoo should be an animals' home, not an animals' prison. Every detail of our zoo (as with the first one the Doctor had shown me long ago) was worked out with this idea foremost in mind, that the animals should be made comfortable and happy. Many of the old things were kept the same. For example, the latches to the houses were all on the inside, so that the animals could come in and go out when they chose. Latch-keys were given out (if a tenant wanted one) when a house or room or hole was let. There were certain rules, it is true, although the Doctor was not fond of rules, but they were all drawn up to protect the animals against one another, rather than to enslave them or cut off their liberty in any way. For instance, anyone wishing to give a party had to notify his next-door neighbour (they were very close, of course); and no tenant was allowed to sing comic songs after midnight.

5

ANIMAL TOWN

ONE of the greatest difficulties the Doctor had in all his dealings with the Animal Kingdom was that of keeping anything secret. But then, I suppose, when we remember how hard it is for people to keep secrets, that need not be so surprising. Polynesia, as soon as I told her about the idea of the new zoo, immediately warned me.

'Keep this to yourself, now, Tommy, as long as you can.

If you don't, neither you nor the Doctor will get any peace.'

I certainly kept it to myself. But nevertheless the news leaked out somehow that John Dolittle was reorganizing and enlarging his zoo in order that a lot of new animals might live with him. And then, exactly as Polynesia had prophesied, we were pestered to death morning, noon and night with applications. You would think that all the animals in the world had been waiting the whole of their lives for a chance to get into the Doctor's household.

He at once had it announced that as I was to be the assistant manager of the new zoo all applications must be made through me. But even so, of course, while that did relieve him of a good deal of annoyance, a great many animals who had known him a long time applied to him direct for a home in the new establishment.

And then we had quite a difficult time sending away some of the old tenants. The Doctor had found that for many foreigners the climate of Puddleby was quite unsuitable. There were a pair of beavers, for example, who had been ill a good deal and quite noticeably out of condition almost the whole time. But they were so attached to the Doctor that although he had often suggested sending them back to Canada they had always politely but stubbornly declined. However, on the Doctor's return this time he found them in such poor health he decided it would be kinder to be firm.

'Listen,' he said to them, 'you may not know it, but this climate is very, very bad for you. It is either not cold enough or not dry enough – or something. I can't have you throwing your health away like this out of mere sentiment. You've *got* to go back to Canada.'

Well, the beavers just burst into tears, both of them. And it was not until John Dolittle had promised them that they should come back after two years – if at the end

of that time they still wanted to – that they were consoled and consented to go.

It was part of my duties as assistant manager to secure the beavers' passage back to Canada. This was no simple matter, as you can easily imagine, because, of course, I could not just hand them over to anyone. I spent several days around the docks of Tilbury before I found a ship's steward whose references for honesty and reliability were such as to satisfy the Doctor. For a certain sum of money he agreed to take them to Halifax on his ship's next voyage to Nova Scotia and to let them go at the mouth of a river well outside the limits of the town.

Not only were there many applications from single

animals and families of animals for accommodations in our zoo, but as soon as it got abroad that John Dolittle was going to set up his long-promised Rat and Mouse Club every other species of animal on earth, it seemed to me, sent committees to him to ask couldn't they have a club, too.

'I told you what it would be like,' said Polynesia, as she and I were pondering one day over a map of the new zoo which I had laid out. 'If the space you had was ten times as big you couldn't accommodate them all.'

'But look here,' said the white mouse (it was most amusing to see how important he had become now that he was being consulted in the Doctor's schemes), 'suppose we set out on your drawing here all the different establishments, private houses, flats, hotels, clubs and what not, then we can see better how much room there is left and how many clubs we can have.'

'Yes,' I said, 'that's a good idea, because once we get the zoo running it will be very hard to dig things out and change them around afterwards. The animals would very naturally object to that.'

'And then I think we ought to have some shops,' said the white mouse. 'Don't you?'

'Shops!' I cried. 'What on earth for?'

'Well, you see,' said he, 'by the time we're finished it will be like a town, anyhow – an animal town – with a principal street, I suppose, and the houses and clubs either side. A few shops where the squirrels could buy nuts and the mice could get acorns and grains of wheat – don't you see? – it would liven things up a bit. Nothing cheers a town up so much as good shops. And I think a restaurant or two where we could go and get our meals if we came home late and hadn't time to get our own supper – yes, that's a good notion – we should surely have a restaurant or two.'

'But who are you going to get to run these shops?' asked Polynesia. 'Stores and cafés don't run themselves, you know.'

'Oh, that's easy,' laughed the white mouse. 'I know lots of mice – and rats, too – who would jump at the chance to run a nut store or a restaurant – just have a natural gift for business, especially catering.'

'Maybe, for the rats and mice,' said Polynesia. 'But they're not the only ones in the zoo, remember. This isn't just a rat and mouse town.'

'Well, I imagine it will probably separate itself into districts, anyway,' said the white mouse. 'You won't forget, Tommy, that you've promised us the top end, near the gate, for our club? I have that whole section laid out in my mind's eye complete. And it is going to be just the neatest little neighbourhood you ever saw.'

Well, after a tremendous amount of planning and working out we finally got the new zoo going. The list of public institutions with which it began was as follows: The Rabbits' Apartment House (this consisted of an enormous mound full of rabbit holes with a common lettuce garden attached), the Home for Cross-Bred Dogs, the Rat and Mouse Club, the Badgers' Tavern, the Foxes' Meeting House and the Squirrels' Hotel.

Each of these was a sort of club in its way. And we had to be most particular about limiting the membership, because from the outset thousands of creatures of each kind wanted to join. The best we could do for those who were not taken in was to keep their names on a waiting list, and as members left (which was very seldom) admit them one by one. Each club had its president and committee who were responsible for the proper organization and orderly carrying on of the establishment.

As the white mouse had prophesied, our new animal town within the high walls of the old bowling green did naturally divide itself up into districts. And the animals from each, while they often mingled in the street with those from other quarters of the town, minded their own business, and no one interfered with anybody else.

This we had to make the first and most important rule of the Dolittle Zoo: within the walls of the town all hunting was forbidden. No member of the Home for Cross-Bred Dogs was allowed to go ratting – in the zoo. No fox was permitted to chase birds or squirrels.

And it was surprising how, when the danger of pursuit by their natural enemies was removed, all the different

sorts of animals took up a new, freer and more open kind of life. For instance, it was no unusual thing in Animal Town to see a mother squirrel lolling on her veranda, surrounded by her children, while a couple of terriers walked down the street within a yard of them.

The shops and restaurants, of course, were mostly patronized by the rats and mice, who had a natural love for city life, and the majority of them were situated in the section at the north end of the enclosure which came to be known as Mouse Town. Nevertheless at the main grocery on a Saturday night we often saw foxes and dogs and crows, all mixed up, buying their Sunday dinner from a large rat. And the mouse errand boys who delivered goods at the customers' houses were not afraid to walk right into a bulldog's kennel or a fox's den.

6

POVERTY AGAIN

OF course it would be quite too much to expect that with lots of different kinds of animals housed in the same enclosure there would be no quarrels or disputes. It was in fact part of the Doctor's plan to see what could be done in getting different creatures who were born natural enemies to live together in harmony.

'Obviously, Stubbins,' said he, 'we can't expect foxes to give up their taste for spring chickens, or dogs their love of ratting, all in a moment. My hope is that by getting them to agree to live peaceably together while within my zoo, we will tend toward a better understanding among them permanently.'

Yes, there *were* fights, especially in the first few months before the different communities got settled down. But, curiously enough, many of the quarrels were among animals of the same kind. I think the badgers were the worst. In the evenings at their tavern they used to play games. Neither the Doctor nor I could ever make out what these games were about. One was played with stones on a piece of ground marked out with scratches. It was almost like drafts or checkers. The badgers used to take this game quite seriously – the badger is rather a heavy type of personality, anyway. And there seemed to be championships played and great public interest taken in the outcome of matches. Frequently these ended in a quarrel. And in the middle of the night a frightened squirrel would come and wake me or the Doctor and tell us there was a fight going on in the Badgers' Tavern and the whole town was being disturbed.

In the end, at the white mouse's suggestion (he was more proud and important than ever, now that he had been elected first Mayor of Animal Town), this led to the Doctor instituting the Zoo Police Force. Two dogs, two foxes, two squirrels, two rabbits and two rats were elected as constables, with a bulldog for captain and a fox as head of the Secret Service. After that woe betide a quarrelsome member who tried to start a brawl in the Badgers' Tavern! He promptly found himself being trotted down the street under arrest to spend the night in the town jail.

One of the first arrests to be made by the zoo police was that of poor Gub-Gub. Having noticed that the vegetable garden attached to the Rabbits' Apartment House was promising a nice harvest of early lettuce, he made a descent on it one night secretly. But the chief of the fox detectives spotted him and he was handcuffed (or trotter-cuffed) before he could say Jack Robinson. It was only on the Doctor's forbidding him entrance to the zoo compound for the future and going security for his good behaviour that he was dismissed the following morning with a caution.

'Next time,' said his honour the Mayor (the white mouse who was acting as magistrate), 'we will give you six days' hard labour in the rabbits' garden – with a muzzle on.'

Besides the Rat and Mouse Club, of which I shall speak further later on, the other more important department in the new zoo was the Home for Cross-Bred Dogs. This was an institution which Jip had long pestered John Dolittle to establish. Ever since the days of the Canary Opera, when Jip had tried to run a Dogs' Free Bone Kitchen in the East End of London, he had been hoping that the Doctor would

discover a way to give all the strays and outcasts of dog-dom a decent home. Now, in the seventh heaven of contentment, he, with Toby and Swizzle, was very busy working out the details of the new club.

'Now some dogs,' said Jip to me, 'like to live in kennels – prefer to be private, you know – and others like to live in houses. So we'll have to have a lot of kennels and at least one good house.'

Thereupon he persuaded me and Bumpo to build a house according to his, Swizzle's and Toby's directions. Toby, always a fussy, bossy little dog, had a whole heap of ideas, mostly for the benefit of the small dogs who were to come. You would think they were surely the most important. And when we finally had it finished I am bound to say the Dogs' House was quite an unusual building. All doors were made to open just with a lift of the nose-latch and a push. The fireplaces were built especially wide, so that at least a dozen dogs could find room to lie in front of each one. All sofas (of which there were many) were made low enough so that the smallest dogs could jump up on to them with ease, and were furnished with special oil-cloth upholstery and cushions, so that they could be easily cleaned if they got muddied up with dirty paws. Drinking bowls were to be found in every room. It was against the rules to leave bones lying around the floor, but a bone-rack (rather like an umbrella stand) was provided for the members near the front door. And here the dogs could leave their bones on going out and find them again on coming in – if they hadn't been borrowed in the meantime.

Meals were served in a special dining-room, where dishes were set out on very low tables; and a grand sideboard buffet with steps to it, where members could go up and make their own choice of cold meats, was an important and popular feature. This department – the supplying of bones and meat to the dogs' kitchen – Matthew Mugg took charge of. Matthew considered himself an expert in dogs, and this side of the zoo held great interest for him.

There there was a special sort of dogs' gymnasium, which Jip called the Roughhouse Room. It had trapezes, balls hung on strings and other special apparatus for dog exercise and dog gymnastics. And here wonderful wrestling contests, tug-o'-war matches, tag games, and sham fights were staged almost every night. The Doctor, Bumpo and I were often invited down to see these sports, which were very good fun to watch, as were also the races and leaping contests which Jip arranged in the dogs' gymnasium.

The Home for Cross-Bred Dogs was, I think, one of the happiest institutions that John Dolittle ever established. Of course, as the Doctor had said, there was to begin with a long list of dogs who had always wanted to be attached to his household. Among these almost the first to turn up at the club were Grab the bulldog and Blackie the retriever, whom John Dolittle had rescued from Harris's animal shop a long time ago.

But in addition to this class there was the much greater number of Jip's friends and acquaintances. Naturally a very charitable dog, Jip loved to go out and hunt round the streets for homeless vagabonds. Every day he would bring home one or two, till very soon the club had about as

many members as it would hold. And even when the Doctor told him he would have to stop, he would, if he found a particularly deserving case, as he called it, sneak in with him after dark and see that at least he got a square meal off the sideboard buffet and a night's lodging. From the outside the gate to the zoo could only be opened by a secret latch. This was worked by pulling a string carefully hidden in a ditch. All members of the zoo were specially instructed in this by the Doctor and made to promise not to give the secret away. And I am bound to say they were very conscientious about it. During the whole of the zoo's career no outsider ever learned the secret of the gate. But when Jip brought his 'deserving cases' home after dark he always made them turn their backs while he pulled the secret latch-string.

As soon as it became known in dog society that John Dolittle had formed a club many dogs who had perfectly good homes of their own just left them and came here – for no other reasons than that they preferred living with the Doctor and because they loved the gymnasium and the good company. And more than one angry owner called at the Doctor's house and was all for having him arrested because, he said, he had lured his dog away from him.

Of course the cost of the upkeep of the new zoo was considerable, especially for the supply of food for the Home for Cross-Bred Dogs. And about six weeks after it had been established Dab-Dab and Too-Too came to me, both looking very serious.

'It is just as I thought it would be,' squawked Dab-Dab, throwing out her wings in a gesture of despair. 'We are already practically at the end of our money again. I don't know how many thousand pesetas it was you brought back with you, but it's nearly all gone. Too-Too and I have been going over accounts and we calculate we have about enough to last for another week. Jip has no sense. The Doctor is bad enough himself, goodness knows, the way he spends money – just regardless. But nobody in the world would be rich enough to keep all the stray mongrels Jip has been bringing in the last few weeks. Well, here we are, penniless again. I don't know what we're going to do, I'm sure.'

7

THE BADGER'S TOOTH

OF course, when I came (with Dab-Dab, Too-Too, and Polynesia) to the Doctor to report the condition of the family bank account he, as usual, took the matter very lightly.

'Don't bother me with such things now,' he said. 'Some money will come in somehow, I have no doubt – it generally does. I'm dreadfully busy.'

But though we managed to collect a few pounds which were due him from people who published his books on natural history, that did not last us long. And soon we were as badly off as ever. Dab-Dab was terribly angry and kept insisting that the Doctor get rid of the zoo, which was almost as expensive to run as all the rest of the household put together.

But John Dolittle was right; something did turn up, and, curiously enough, it turned up inside the zoo itself and saved that institution from extinction as well as the Dolittle household from bankruptcy. This is how it happened: one night, just as the Doctor was going to bed after a hard day's work with his new book on oceanography, a member of the Badgers' Tavern knocked on the door asking to see him. He said he had a terrible toothache and wanted the Doctor, if he would, to look at it at once. This, of course, the Doctor did. He was very clever at animal dentistry.

'Ah!' said he. 'You've broken a corner off that tooth. No wonder it hurts. But it can be stopped. Open your mouth a little wider, please. . . . That's better – why, how curious! Did I ever fill any teeth for you before ?'

'No,' said the badger. 'This is the first time I've come to you for treatment of any kind. I'm very healthy.'

'But you have gold in your teeth,' said the Doctor. 'How did that come there if you haven't been to some dentist?'

'I'm sure I don't know,' said the badger. 'What is gold?'

'Look, I'll show you in the mirror,' said the Doctor. 'Stubbins, give me that hand-glass, will you, please?'

I got it and brought it to the Doctor, who held it in front of the badger's face while he pointed to a place in his teeth with a small instrument.

'There,' said John Dolittle, 'you see that yellow metal sticking between your teeth? That's gold.'

'Oh!' said the badger, peering into the mirror, very

pleased with his own handsome reflection. 'I and my wife were digging a hole out by Dobbin's Meadow and we chewed up a whole lot of that stuff. That's what I broke my tooth on.'

Polynesia, who was in the surgery at the time, was more interested in this statement of the badger's than was the Doctor. She flew across the room and from one of her hanging rings she peered into the animal's open mouth where John Dolittle was at work on the broken tooth. Then she came back to me and whispered :

'Well, of all things! He's been eating gold. *Eating* it, mind you – and us as poor as church mice. Tommy, we will speak with this gentleman as soon as the Doctor has done with him.'

John Dolittle did not take long over making his patient comfortable. In spite of his podgy fat hands he had the quickest and nimblest fingers in the world.

'I have put a dressing in your tooth which will stop the pain for the present, and you'll have to come back and see me again tomorrow,' he said as the badger closed his mouth and waddled down off the table. 'You must be careful what you chew up when you're digging holes. No teeth will stand biting on metal, you know – not even yours. Good night.'

As the patient left the surgery Polynesia made a sign to me, and we followed him.

'Where did you say you were digging this hole?' asked Polynesia as we walked beside him toward the zoo enclosure.

'Over near Dobbin's Meadow,' said the badger; 'just a bit to the north of it. We were tunnelling into a bank – as much for exercise as anything else. It was a cold day. But we did hope we might find some pig nuts. Also, we need a refuge hole or two up in that direction. Some of these dogs the Doctor has here in such numbers now are getting much too cheeky. They never touch us while we are in the zoo, it is true, but if they get wind of us when we're outside they think it is funny to chase us all over the landscape. Our committee down at the Badgers' Tavern thought we ought to have a refuge hole up in that neighbourhood.'

'What is a refuge hole?' I asked.

'Oh, it's just a public hole,' said he. 'We have them stuck around all over the place. But we all know where they are. They're just holes where any badger can take refuge if chased by dogs. We dig them very deep, and sometimes provision them with food in case the dogs should besiege us for a long time. We have to protect ourselves, you know. Our pace is slow.'

'Well, now, look here,' said Polynesia, as we reached the zoo gate, 'Tommy and I would like to make an appointment with you for tomorrow morning early – very early. We want to see this place where you broke your tooth. Suppose we meet you at the north end of Dobbin's Meadow at, say, five o'clock.'

'All right,' said the badger. 'But that isn't early for me. This time of year it has been broad daylight for more than a quarter of an hour by five. We don't go by the clock, you know; we go by the sun. We prefer to travel before dawn. I'll meet you there at daybreak.'

The following morning Polynesia had me out of bed and dressing by candle-light before the cocks had given their first crow.

'But don't you see, Tommy,' said she, in answer to my sleepy grumbling at this unearthly hour for rising, 'it's frightfully important that we get there and do what exploring is necessary before there are people about.'

I found it hard to be enthusiastic, even over the prospect of discovering gold, so early.

'But what are you expecting to find?' I asked. 'Do you fancy that old badger has run into a mine? There aren't any gold mines in England.'

'I've no more idea than you have,' said she impatiently. 'But just because no gold mines have been discovered so far, that doesn't mean that none ever will be. The fact remains that that blessed animal ran into gold of some kind, or he wouldn't have it sticking in his teeth. Hurry up and get your coat on. I think I see the dawn beginning to show in the east.'

Downstairs Polynesia made me collect a spade from the tool shed and the Doctor's mineral hammer from his study before we started away through the chilly morning twilight for Dobbin's Meadow.

The old badger was there, sure enough, waiting for us. And he promptly lumbered off alongside a hedge to lead us to the place where he had dug the hole. This, when we came to it, proved not to be in the Dobbin property at all, but on the other side of the hedge, in a wide, open piece of heathland, known as Puddleby Common. It was a territory I knew well. Many a time I had hunted over this semi-wild region for birds' nests, mushrooms, and blackberries. Here, too, I had often watched with fascination the Gipsy folk pitching their tents and lighting their fires. For this was common ground from which no man had the right to turn them off.

8

THE PUDDLEBY GOLD RUSH

'THIS is lucky,' whispered Polynesia as we came to a halt before the hole which the badger had dug. 'Puddleby Common, public property – don't you see, Tommy? Even if anyone does see us digging here they can't stop us. Just the same, we must not give the show away. Get your spade now and go to work.'

I was still very sleepy. But little by little the fascination of hunting in the earth for treasure took hold of me. And before long I was working away as though my life depended on it, and, despite the chill of the morning air, the perspiration was running down my forehead in streams and I had to stop often and dry it off.

We had explained to the badger what we were after, and his assistance was very helpful. He began by going down to the bottom of the hole and bringing up several

shapeless pieces of gravelly metal. These, when I cut into
them with a penknife, showed the soft yellow gold of
which they were composed.

'That's the piece I broke my tooth on,' said the badger –
'and it is the last of it. Is the stuff any good?'

'Why, my gracious!' said Polynesia, 'of course it is.
That's what they make money out of – sovereigns. Are
you sure this is all there is? If we can get enough we have
made the Doctor a rich man for life.'

The badger went back and dug the hole still deeper, and
with my spade I cut away the bank all around and levelled
out tons of gravel, which we searched and raked over
diligently. But not another nugget could we find.

'Well, just the same,' said Polynesia, inspecting the array of pieces which I had laid out on my open handkerchief, 'we have a tidy little fortune as it is. Now let's get away before anyone sees what we've been up to.'

When we told the Doctor about it at breakfast he was much more interested in it from the geological, the scientific point of view, than he was from that of money or profit.

'It is most extraordinary,' he said, examining the specimens I had brought home in the handkerchief. 'If you had found old gold coins it would not have been so surprising. But these look like nuggets – native gold. Geologically, this is something quite new for England. I would like to see the place where you found it.'

'In the meantime,' said Dab-Dab, 'leave these nuggets with me, will you? I know a safe place to keep them till we can turn them into cash.'

When the Doctor set out with me and Polynesia to examine the place where the gold had been found, Jip and Gub-Gub, though they had not been invited, came along too.

Our prospecting exploration was very thorough. We searched the whole length of that gravel bank, digging and sifting and testing. Gub-Gub caught the fever, and Jip, too. They burrowed into the slope like regular prospectors, Gub-Gub using his nose as though he were digging for truffles and Jip scraping out the earth with his front paws the way he always did when he was going after rats.

But we found no more gold.

'It's very puzzling,' said the Doctor, 'very. Quite a geological mystery. This is not really gold-bearing gravel at all. And yet that gold is exactly as it would be found *in* gravel – in nugget form. The only explanation I can think of is that it was dug up elsewhere by some very early miners and then buried here for safe keeping.'

But if we were not successful in finding a real gold mine, we were successful in starting a prospecting boom. By the time the Doctor had finished his survey of the ground it was quite late in the morning. As we left the Common and started on our way home we noticed that one or two people had been watching us. Later we questioned Matthew Mugg and Bumpo, who had accompanied the expedition, and they swore they never told anyone. Nevertheless, it apparently leaked out that gold had been found in a gravel bank on Puddleby Common. And by four o'clock that afternoon the place was crowded with people armed with picks, shovels, garden trowels, firetongs – every imaginable implement – all hunting for gold.

The whole of Puddleby had gone prospecting mad. Nursemaids with perambulators left their charges to bawl while they scratched in the ground with buttonhooks and shoehorns for gold. Loafers, poachers, gipsies, pedlars, the town tradesmen, respectable old gentlemen, school children – they came from all ranks and classes.

One rumour had it that the Doctor had discovered a lot of ancient Roman goblets, made of gold, and several old saucepans and kettles were dug up by the prospectors and taken away to be tested to see what they were made of.

After the second day the poor Common looked as though a cyclone or an earthquake had visited it. And the Town Council said they were going to prosecute the Doctor for the damage he had brought to public property.

For over a week the gold boom continued. People came from outside, real mining experts from London, to look into this strange rumour which had set everyone agog.

Gub-Gub, who of all the Doctor's household had the prospecting fever the worst, could hardly be kept away from the Common. He was sure he had found his real profession at last.

'Why,' said he, 'I can dig better holes with my nose than any of those duffers can with a spade – and quicker.'

He kept begging to be allowed to go back to continue the hunt. He was so afraid these other people might any minute discover a real mine which ought to be the property of the Dolittle household.

'You need not be worried, Gub-Gub,' said the Doctor. 'It isn't a mineral-bearing gravel at all. The gold we got came there by accident. The badger was probably right – there is no more than just that little hoard, which must have been specially buried there ages and ages ago.'

But Gub-Gub, while the boom continued, was not to be dissuaded, and his mining fever got worse rather than

better. When the Doctor would not allow him to go back to the Common (he went several times secretly at night) he consoled himself by prospecting in the kitchen garden for mushrooms. He even brought his new profession to the table with him and went prospecting for raisins in the rice pudding.

By whatever means the gold had come, Dab-Dab was very pleased that Polynesia's business-like attention had secured it all for the Doctor. Left to himself he would most likely not have profited by it at all. The Town Council insisted that he give it up as Crown property. And this he willingly consented to do. But the wily Matthew Mugg consulted a solicitor and found that under ancient law the finder was entitled to half of it. Even this sum, when the gold was weighed, proved to be quite considerable.

'Well,' sighed Dab-Dab, 'as the Doctor would say, "it's an ill wind that blows nobody any good." That old badger breaking his tooth was a stroke of luck. It was just in time. I really didn't know where the next meal was coming from. Now, thank goodness, we shan't have to worry about the bills for another six months, anyhow.'

9

THE MOUSE CODE

THERE had been a good deal of anxiety for some time past in the various departments of the zoo over Dab-Dab's constant demand that the Doctor should close the whole place up. Seeing how expensive it was to run, her argument sounded reasonable enough, and the members had all felt a bit selfish over continuing their clubs and other institutions when the cost was such a burden to the Doctor.

So with the news that half of the treasure found on the Common had been awarded to John Dolittle by the courts, the greatest rejoicing broke out in Animal Town – all the way from the Home for Cross-Bred Dogs at one end to the Rat and Mouse Club at the other. Even the timid pushmi-pullyu, who had now made his home within the peaceful, pleasant retirement of the zoo enclosure, joined in the jubilation, as did what few foreigners we still had, like the Russian minks and the Canadian woodchucks. I never heard such a pandemonium in my life. The information was brought to the zoo about supper time by Toby and Swizzle. Immediately a demonstration began in every quarter. All the citizens spilled out of the clubs into the street cheering,

or making noises which to them were the same as cheering.

'The Doctor's rich again!' passed from mouth to mouth, from door to door. The mixture of barks, squeals, grunts and squawks was so extraordinary that a policeman, passing on the Oxenthorpe Road outside, knocked at the Doctor's door and asked if everything was all right.

A little later the animals began organizing parades and went walking up and down the main street of Animal Town singing what they called songs. The white mouse, as Mayor of the town, was in charge – frightfully important – and he suggested, as it was now quite dark, that Mousetown should have a torchlight procession. He asked me to get a box of those very small candles which they put on birthday cakes and Christmas trees. Then he insisted that I should fix up a banner with 'Hooray! The Doctor's Rich Again!' on it in large letters. And fifty-four mice and fifty-four rats formed themselves up, two by two, each pair carrying a candle, and they marched round Mousetown from eight o'clock till midnight, singing the most extraordinary songs you ever heard. Every once in a while they would come to a halt and yell in chorus: 'Hooray! The Doctor's rich again! – Hooray! Hooray!'

A little extra excitement was added when one pair of torchbearers had an accident with their candle and set light to the Squirrels' Hotel. And as that building was largely made of dry leaves it not only burned to the ground in no time at all, but very nearly set the whole zoo in flames as well.

However, no one was injured (the squirrels were all out celebrating), and after the entire town had formed itself into a fire brigade the blaze was quickly put out. Then every one set to on the work of reconstruction and the Squirrels' Hotel was rebuilt in a night.

'It was a grand occasion,' declared the white mouse when it was all over. 'And the bonfire was almost the best part of it.'

Indeed, the white mouse was naturally of a cheerful, pleasure-loving disposition. And after the success of this first celebration he was continually wanting to organize club parties, city fêtes, processions, and entertainments of one kind or another. This, while the Doctor was always glad to see the animals enjoying themselves, could not be encouraged too far, because a lot of noise was usually a most important part of Animal Town festivities. And although the zoo stood well within the Doctor's own land, the racket which the Home for Cross-Bred Dogs made on these occasions could be heard miles away.

Many new and interesting features developed quite naturally in the zoo, for example, the Animals' Free Library. Shortly after I had visited my parents on our return from abroad, the Doctor had asked me to try to organize and arrange the tremendous quantity of material which he had collected and written on animal language. He had one whole bedroom above his study simply packed with books, manuscript notes and papers on this subject. It was all in great disorder, and the task of getting it straightened out was a heavy one.

But Polynesia and the white mouse helped me. We got Matthew Mugg to make us a lot of bookcases. And after a week of sorting and cataloguing and listing we had arranged the extraordinary collection in something like order. I think it was a surprise even to the Doctor himself, when we finally invited him into the little room above the study and showed him the bookshelves running all round the walls, to realize what a tremendous amount of work he had done on the science of animal languages.

'Why, Doctor,' squeaked the white mouse, gazing round the shelves, 'this is a regular animal library you have here! It ought to be down in the zoo, where the animals could make use of it, instead of here.'

'Yes, there's something in that,' said the Doctor. 'But most of these writings of mine are only *about* animal languages – dictionaries and so forth – very few are actually story books written *in* animal language. And then, besides, so few of you can read, anyway.'

'Oh, but we could soon learn,' said the white mouse. 'If you got one or two of us taught we could quickly teach the rest. Oh, I do think an important institution like the Rat and Mouse Club ought to have a library of its own. Yes, indeed!'

Well, in spite of the objection which the Doctor had

HUGH LOFTING

advanced, the white mouse stuck to his idea of an Animal
Public Library for the Dolittle Zoo. He pointed out that so
far as the rats and mice were concerned (and the dogs,
badgers and squirrels, too, for that matter) there was
nothing they enjoyed so much as stories.

'I would be delighted to do it for you,' said the Doctor,
'but in rat and mouse talk, for instance, there are no letters
– there *is* no written language.'

'But we can soon invent one, can't we?' asked the white
mouse. 'Why, there must have been a time when there
wasn't any human written language. Listen, Doctor, you
invent a sign alphabet for mice – simple, you know – we
don't want any physics or skizzics to begin with – and

64

HUGH LOFTING

teach it to me. I'll promise to teach the whole of the Rat and Mouse Club in a week. They're awfully keen about learning new things. What do you say?'

Of course such a suggestion, one might be sure, would always interest John Dolittle, who had given so many years of his life to animal education. He at once set to work and with the white mouse's co-operation devised a simple alphabet in rat and mouse language. There were only ten signs, or letters, in all. The Doctor called it the Mouse Code, but Polynesia and I called it the Squeaker-B-C, because it was all in squeaks of different kinds, and each letter had two different meanings, according as you let your squeak fall or rise at the end.

Then came the business of printing and binding the books. This the doctor turned over to me as soon as he had established the alphabet or code. Of course, the volumes had to be terribly, terribly tiny in order that even the young mice could read and handle them with ease. The white mouse was most anxious that the young folk should be able to take advantage of the new education. What we called our 'Mouse Octavo' size of book was just slightly smaller than a penny postage stamp. The binding had to be all hand-sewn and only the finest thread could be used. The pages were so small that I had to have a watchmakers' magnifying eyeglass to do my printing with, which was, of course, also all hand work. But no matter how tiny the letters were made, they were none too small for mouse eyes, which can pick out single grains of dust with the greatest ease.

We were very proud of our first book printed in mouse language. Although it was mostly the work of the Doctor, I, as printer and publisher, felt just as important as Caxton or Gutenberg as I put the name of my firm into the title page: 'Stubbins & Stubbins. Puddleby-on-the-Marsh' (I didn't know who the second 'Stubbins' was, but I thought it looked better and more business-like that way).

'This is a great occasion, Tommy,' said the white mouse as we officially declared the edition (one copy) off the press. 'The first volume printed in the mouse code! We are making history as well as books.'

THE NEW LEARNING

A s the white mouse had prophesied, the new education was taken up with great enthusiasm by all classes of Rat and Mouse Society. The famous and truly rare first book from the press of Stubbins & Stubbins did not survive to be handed down to posterity. It was torn to shreds in the first week by the zealous public, who thronged the Animal Public Library in the Dolittle Zoo.

For the white mouse had insisted that the book be put into the library, and that institution officially opened with great pomp and ceremony. This was an occasion also for another of his favourite celebrations. But the more serious purpose was to attract public attention in Animal Town toward education and reading generally.

But the rats and mice continued to be the most keen to learn for themselves. There was a mystery about this new art that appealed to their natural inquisitiveness. The others, dogs, badgers, squirrels, foxes and rabbits, were quite content to be read to aloud. And for the first part of its career the Public Library chiefly did duty as a general recreation-room where the white mouse read aloud every afternoon to a mixed and motley company.

The demand for books in the mouse code was enormous. The public, curiously enough, seemed to be very keen about poetry – especially comic poetry. The institution of the Public Library and of the Rat and Mouse Club Library (which was established a little later) seemed to encourage this art tremendously. And many rats and mice who had no idea of being poetic heretofore suddenly, with the new education, blossomed forth into verse.

It became the custom at the restaurant in Mousetown (they called it 'The Stilton Cheese') for rat poets to get up and recite their own ballads to the assembled diners. The audience expressed its opinion of the verse by hooting or cheering. If the poet had a good voice he often sang his ballad, and when it was well received a collection was usually taken up for him by the proprietor. An egg-shell was used as a hat and it was passed round among the tables and the public dropped acorns or grains of barley into it instead of money. Nearly all the mouse poets, as I said, wrote in a cheerful vein and their comic songs were usually the most popular. Often about suppertime if the Doctor and I passed near the zoo wall we would hear shrieks of high-pitched, squeaky laughter; and then we would know that some comic ballad monger was singing his latest lampoon to the gay company at The Stilton Cheese.

Another thing that greatly encouraged the new zest for education was the mouse magazine which the Doctor established. It was called *Cellar Life*, and was issued on the first of every month. This, too, was a semi-comic periodical, and besides giving the latest news and gossip of the zoo, it contained jokes and funny pictures.

Now, on the mantelpiece of the Doctor's old waiting-room, disused ever since he had given up his practice, a miniature had always stood. It was a tiny portrait painted on ivory of John Dolittle as a young man, and for years it had never been moved from its place between the Empire clock and a Dresden china shepherdess. But one day the miniature disappeared and no one could account for it. The Doctor asked Dab-Dab, and that good housekeeper said she had seen it the previous day when she had given the waiting-room its weekly dusting, but had no idea at what hour it had disappeared nor what could have become of it.

The Doctor asked Jip, Too-Too, Chee-Chee, Polynesia and me, but none of us could throw any light on the mystery. John Dolittle valued the picture only because his mother had had it painted by a well-known artist the year he had graduated in medicine. However, he had a great many things to keep him occupied, and after a few more inquiries, which met with no better success, he dismissed the matter from his mind.

It was about two weeks after the opening of the Animal Public Library that the white mouse called on the Doctor one evening, when he and I were busy over a new book he was writing on deep-sea plants.

'I have two things I would like to speak to you about, Doctor,' said the Mayor of Animal Town, gravely stroking his white whiskers. 'One is, I would like to have a book written – in the mouse code, of course, a textbook on mouse traps. We need it – especially for the new generation. Young boy and girl mice wander off from the nest as soon as they get big enough. And before they've had time to learn anything about the world at all they get caught in the first trap that entices them with a piece of mouldy cheese.'

'All right,' said the Doctor. 'I think that can be done – if Stubbins here can make the pictures of the traps small enough to go into a mouse-octavo volume.'

'Oh, it could be done in rat-quarto if necessary,' said the white mouse. 'This is a textbook, you see. And we are going to make it compulsory for all parents who are memers of the club to read it aloud to their children. The accidents from traps this last month have been just appalling. I would like to have every known kind of mouse and rat trap shown. It should be a complete work. Of course, I will help with the writing of it. You will need an expert, an old hand, to describe what the traps smell and look like from a mouse's point of view.'

'Oh, my gracious!' put in Dab-Dab, who was listening down by the fire. 'Then we'll have the whole world overrun with mice. It is too bad we haven't got a few good mouse traps in my linen closet.'

'Yes, but you wouldn't like it if there were duck traps there as well,' the white mouse responded, his whiskers bristling with indignation.

'Well, now, what was the other thing you wanted to see me about?' the Doctor asked.

'The other thing is also very important,' said the white mouse. 'I've come on behalf of the house committee to invite you and Tommy here to our club's Mooniversary Dinner.'

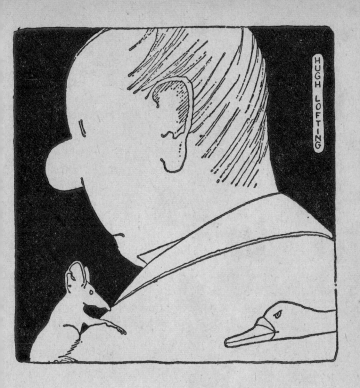

'*Mooniversary!*' the Doctor murmured. 'Er – what does that mean?'

'Yes, it's a new word,' said the white mouse, rather proudly. 'But then all languages have special words, haven't they, which the other languages haven't? So why shouldn't the mouse code have a word or two of its own? It happened this way: the house committee was having a meeting and the Railway Rat – he's one of the members, lived in a railway station, decent fellow, but he smells of kerosene – the Railway Rat got up and proposed that since the club had now been going on successfully for some time we ought to have an anniversary dinner to celebrate.'

71

'You're always celebrating,' muttered Dab-Dab from the fireside.

'Then,' the white mouse continued, 'the Hansom Cab Mouse – he's another member, lived under the floor of an old cab, knows London like a book – he gets up and he says, "Anniversary means a year. The club hasn't been going for a year. A year's a long time in a mouse's life. I suggest we call it the Club's Mooniversary Dinner, to celebrate our month's birthday, not our year's birthday."

'Well, they argued about it a good deal, but the suggestion was finally accepted – that our celebration banquet should be called the Mooniversary Dinner. Then the Church Mouse – he's another member, lived in a church, awful poor, fed on candle wax mostly, kind of religious type, always wants us to sing hymns instead of comic songs – he gets up and he says, "I would like to suggest to the committee that the Mooniversary Dinner would not be complete without the presence of Doctor John Dolittle, through whose untiring efforts" (he rather fancies himself as a speaker, does the Church Mouse – I suppose he's heard an awful lot of sermons) – "through whose untiring efforts," says he, "for the welfare of rat and mouse society this club first came into being. I propose we invite the Doctor to the Mooniversary Dinner – also that strange lad called Thomas Stubbins, who has made a very good assistant manager to the Dolittle Zoo."

'That motion was carried, too, without any question. And they chose me to come and present the club's invitation. The dinner's tomorrow night, Doctor. You won't have to change or anything. Wear just whatever clothes you happen to have on. But say you'll come.'

'Why, of course,' said John Dolittle, 'I shall be delighted – and I'm sure Stubbins will, too.'

II

THE RAT AND MOUSE CLUB

WITHOUT doubt the Rat and Mouse Club was the only building of its kind in the world. At the beginning the clubhouse had been no more than two and a half feet high; but as the list of members had been enlarged, first from fifty to three hundred, and then from three hundred to five thousand, it became necessary to enlarge the premises considerably.

At the time when the Doctor and I were invited to

attend the Mooniversary Dinner the building was about the height of a man and just about as broad – and as long – as it was high. The architecture was very unusual. In shape the clubhouse was rather like a large bee-hive, with a great number of tiny doors. It was fourteen storeys high. The upper floors were reached by outside staircases, in the manner of Italian houses. In the centre of the building, in-side, there was a large chamber called The Assembly Room which ran the entire height of the structure from ground-floor to roof. Ordinarily this was used for concerts, theatri-cals, and for the general meetings of the club when all the members came together to vote on some new proposal or to celebrate birthdays or occasions of importance. The whole thing was thus a sort of thick hollow dome, in the shell of which were the livingrooms, furnished apartments, private dining-saloons, committee-rooms, etc.

The entrances were all, of course, very small – just big enough for a rat to pass through. But for this special occasion the white mouse had got the badgers to dig a tunnel down under the foundations through which the Doctor and I could reach the Assembly Room inside.

When we arrived at the mouth of this tunnel we found the white mouse and a regular committee on hand to greet us. Moreover, every doorway, all the way up the building, was thronged with rat and mouse faces waiting to witness the great man's arrival. After the white mouse, as president of the club, had made a short speech of welcome, we began the descent of the tunnel.

'Be careful how you go, Doctor,' I said. 'If we bump the top of the tunnel with our backs we're liable to throw the whole building over.'

Without mishap we reached the Assembly Room, where there was just about space enough for the two of us to stand upright, very close together. The white mouse said he wanted to show the Doctor over the clubhouse. But of course as none of the rooms, except the one in which we were standing, was big enough for a man to get into, being 'shown over' the building consisted of standing where he was and peering through the tiny holes called doors. Some of the rooms were along passages, and one could not see them direct from the Assembly Room. But to provide for this the white mouse had got me to bring the Doctor's dentist's mirror, so he could poke it down the passages and see into the rooms around the corners, the same as he would look at the back of a person's tooth.

John Dolittle was tremendously interested in examining the tiny rooms which these highly civilized rats and mice had designed, set out and furnished for themselves. For this building with all it contained was (excepting the few things which I and Bumpo had done for them) entirely their own work. The Chief Mouse Architect – he was also the stone-mason – was on hand and he took great pride in pointing out to the distinguished visitor the whys and the wherefores of all the details of design.

While the Doctor was poking round among the passages and holes with his tooth-mirror he suddenly got quite excited.

'Why, Stubbins,' he cried, 'come and look here. I don't know whether I'm dreaming or not. But isn't that a human face I see down there? Look in the mirror. It reminds me of myself.'

I looked into the mirror. Then I laughed.

'No wonder it reminds you of yourself, Doctor,' I said. 'It *is* yourself. That's the missing miniature of John Dolittle as a young man.'

At this moment I heard the white mouse, who had left us for a moment, scolding the architect in whispers behind the Doctor's back.

'Didn't I tell you,' said he furiously, 'to miss the Committee Room and show the Doctor the Ladies' Lounge instead? – Blockhead! Now we'll lose our best painting.'

'But how did the miniature get here?' asked John Dolittle.

'Well,' said the white mouse, 'we didn't exactly steal it, Doctor. It was the Prison Rat's idea – he's one of the members, has always lived in jails, sort of an unscrupulous customer, but has a great sense of humour and knows no end of interesting stories, crime stories. – Well, as I was saying, it was his idea. We were having a meeting about the lay-out of the new Committee Room and how it should be furnished and decorated. You see, although it's small, it is

76

HUGH LOFTING

in a way the most important room in the club. All the big decisions are made there. And some one got up and said we ought to have a picture on the wall over the president's chair. Then the Church Mouse arose and said, "Brethren," says he, "I think we should have a motto there, some message of good counsel, like, '*Love One Another*'." "Well, I don't," said the Prison Rat, short like. "We can love one another all we want without boasting about it or writing it up on the wall." Then the Railway Rat gets up and says, "No, we ought to have a picture there. We don't want any sloppy mottoes. We want something cheerful. Let's put up one of the comic pictures out of *Cellar Life*." At that the Prison Rat gets up again and says, "I believe in being light-

77

hearted, but I think a comic picture is hardly the thing – not – er – dignified enough for our Committee Room. What we ought to have is a portrait of the founder of our club, Doctor John Dolittle – and I know where I can get one, the right size to fit that place." So the motion was carried – and so was the picture, by the Prison Rat who went up to your house that very night and – er – borrowed it off the mantelpiece in your waiting-room. Will you want to take it away again, Doctor?'

'No, I don't suppose so,' said John Dolittle, smiling. 'It looks very well where it is. And it is quite a compliment that you want to keep it there. I will gladly present it to the club, provided you will take care of it. But you had better not let Dab-Dab know.'

'You may be sure we won't,' said the white mouse. 'And now, Doctor, if you and Tommy will take your seats I will call in the members who are all waiting for the signal to assemble. We had to keep the hall clear till you got seated because, as you will see for yourself, there isn't very much room.'

Thereupon the Doctor and I sort of folded ourselves up and sat down in the cramped space to this strangest banquet table that ever was laid. Our chairs were empty biscuit-tins borrowed from the Home for Cross-Bred Dogs. The table was egg-shaped, about three feet across and five feet long. The dishes, tiny little messes of cheese, nuts, dried fish, fried bread-crumbs, apple-seeds, the kernels of prune-stones, etc., were all gathered in the centre of the table, leaving a large outside ring clear for the diners to sit on. For in Mousetown one always sat, or stood, on the table at meal-times, even in the best society.

As soon as we were seated the white mouse gave a signal somewhere and then a very curious thing happened: hundreds and thousands of rats and mice suddenly poured out

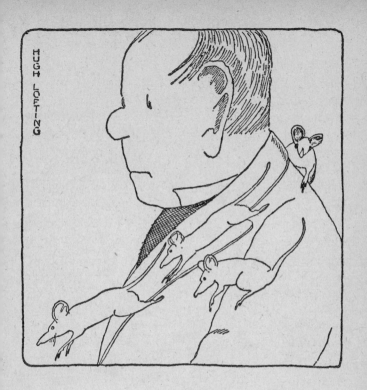

of holes all around us, squeaking and squealing with glee.

'You must excuse them, Doctor,' whispered the president, as a dozen rats ran around John Dolittle's collar and down his sleeve on to the table. 'Their manners are not usually so atrocious. I expected a rush for the places nearest to you – it is a great honour for them, you know, they want to boast that they sat beside you – that's why I kept them out till you were seated. Every single member of the club bought a ticket for the dinner – five thousand, you see, as well as some extra guests from out of town. So you mustn't mind a little crowding.'

12

THE MOONIVERSARY DINNER

THE Mooniversary Dinner was a very great success. Of course neither the Doctor nor I could say afterwards that we had dined heartily. There was a vast number of dishes, it was true; but the plates were only walnut-shells, and clearly it would need a tremendous number of helpings of that size to make a square meal for a man. The drinks were served in acorn-cups.

However, the banquet was so interesting and unusual in other respects that neither of us noticed very much whether we were hungry or not. To begin with, it was quite a novel sensation to be dining, shut up in a room into which we only just fitted, with five thousand rats and mice. Once we got seated and the scramble for places near the great man was over, the members were very well-behaved. There were two sets of waiters, one on the table and the other off the table. Those on the table carried the dishes from the centre to the diners, who had seated themselves in a ring about twenty deep around the edge. The other lot were kept busy swarming up and down the legs of the table, running between the kitchen and the Assembly Room to replenish the supply of such dishes as ran out.

'More apple seeds up!' the head waiter on the table would yell. And a couple of mice down below would hustle off to the kitchen, where the cooks would give them an egg-shell full of apple seeds to bring to the table. It was all excellently managed. The kitchen staff was kept very busy; for although a mouse or rat may not eat a great deal at one meal, when you have five thousand diners to feed it means considerable work.

At one of the upper doorways a small mouse orchestra played tunes throughout the dinner. Their instruments were invented by themselves and consisted of drums of different kinds and shapes and harps made by stretching threads across nutshells. One mouse had a straw which he played in the manner of a flute. Their idea of music was rather peculiar and very faint – indeed with the enormous chatter of squeaky conversation going on all around they could hardly be heard at all.

When the last course had been finished the white mouse knocked on the table for silence. Immediately the chorus of conversation died down and several members shooed the waiters who were making a noise clearing away the walnut-shells and acorn-cups. Finally, after the door into the pantry had been stopped up with a banana skin to keep out the clatter of the washing-up, His Honour the Mayor, First President of the Rat and Mouse Club, cleared his throat with a dignified cough and began a very fine after-dinner speech.

I was sorry afterwards that I had never learned shorthand so that I could have taken down the white mouse's address word for word; for it was in its way the most remarkable I have ever listened to.

He began by telling the Doctor on behalf of the whole club how glad they were to see him seated at their board. Then he turned back to the vast throng of members and sketched out briefly what John Dolittle had done for mouse civilization and what it was to be hoped his efforts would lead to in the future.

'The majority of men,' said he, 'would never believe it if they were told of the general advance, organization and culture which this club, through Doctor John Dolittle, has brought into rat and mouse society.' (Cries of 'Hear, hear!') 'This is the first time in history that our great race has been given a chance to show what it could do.' (The white mouse pounded the table with his tiny fist and grew quite earnest and eloquent.) 'What has our life always been heretofore?' he asked. 'Why, getting chased, being hunted – flight, concealment, that was our daily lot. Through the Doctor's far-sightedness the rat and mouse peoples have here, in Animal Town, been able to think of other things besides keeping out of the jaws of a cat or a dog or a trap. And, I ask you, what has been the result?'

The president paused and for a silent second twirled his white whiskers, while his spellbound audience sat breathless, waiting for him to go on.

'Why, this,' he continued, waving his hand round the

lofty walls of the Assembly Room: 'this great institution called the Rat and Mouse Club; your education; the education of your children; all the things which our new civilization has given us, these are the results which John Dolittle has brought into rat and mouse society by removing the constant anxiety of our lives and giving us comfortable peace and honest freedom in its place. I, myself, look forward – as, I am sure, you all do – to the time when rat and mouse civilization shall be at least on a level with that of Man; to the time when there shall be rat and mouse cities all over the world, rat and mouse railway trains, steamship lines, universities, and grand opera. I propose that we give the Doctor, who has honoured us with his presence here tonight, a vote of thanks to express our appreciation of all he has done for the welfare of rats and mice.'

At the conclusion of the president's speech a great tumult broke loose. Every single one of the five thousand members sprang to his feet, cheering and waving, to show that he agreed with the sentiments of the speaker. And I could see that the Doctor was quite affected by the extraordinary demonstration in his honour.

There was a slight pause, during which it became quite evident that the guest of honour was expected to make some kind of an address in reply. So rising with great care lest he wreck his hosts' clubhouse, John Dolittle made a short speech which was also received with great applause.

Then followed a considerable number of personal introductions. Of course the Doctor knew many members of the club personally. But hundreds of rats and mice who had never met him were now clamouring to be presented to the great man.

Among those who came forward there were some very interesting characters. First there were those whom the white mouse had already spoken of to the Doctor: the Prison Rat, the Church Mouse, the Railway Rat and the Hansom Cab Mouse. But besides these there were many more. They did not all live permanently at the club. Several used to drop in there two or three times a week, usually in the evening, and then go back again to their regular homes about midnight. And there were some who came from quite a long way off attracted by the reputation of this extraordinary establishment, which was now getting to be known all over the country.

For instance, there was the Museum Mouse, who had made his home in a natural history museum up in London and who had travelled all the way down from the city (the Railway Rat had put him on a goods train which he knew

was coming to a town near Puddleby) just to be present at this important banquet. He was a funny little fellow who knew a whole lot about natural history and what new animals were being stuffed by the museum professors. John Dolittle was very interested in the news he brought with him from the scientific world of London.

Then there was the Zoo Rat who had also come from London especially for the occasion. He lived in the Zoological Gardens in Regent's Park, and boasted that he had often been into the lion's den – when the lion was asleep – to steal suet. There was the Tea-house Mouse, the Volcano Rat and the Ice-box Mouse (who had very long fur which he had specially grown from living constantly in cold temperatures). Then there was the Ship's Rat, the same old fellow who had warned the Doctor at the Canary Islands about the rottenness of the ship he was travelling in. He had now retired permanently from the sea and come to settle down in Puddleby to club life and a peaceful old age. There was the Hospital Mouse and the Theatre Mouse and several more.

Of course, with so many, it was only possible for the Doctor to talk a few moments to each. But as the president brought them up and briefly told us who they were, I realized that an assembly of rats and mice could be just as interesting, if you knew about their lives and characters, as any gathering of distinguished people.

13

THE HOTEL RAT

WHEN most of the introductions were over the Doctor surprised me (as he often did) by his remarkable and accurate memory for animal faces. Out of the thousands of rats and mice who were all staring at him in rapt admiration he suddenly pointed to one and whispered to the white mouse:

'Who is that rat over there – the one rubbing the side of his nose with his left paw?'

'That's the Hotel Rat,' said the white mouse. 'Did you want to speak to him?'

But the rat in question had already noticed the Doctor pointing to him and, most proud to be recognized, came forward.

'Your face is very familiar,' said the Doctor. 'I have been wondering where I saw it before.'

HUGH LOFTING

'Oh, I'm the rat who was brought to you half dead, you recollect? About four years ago. My two brothers' had to wake you up at six in the morning. It was an urgent case. I was quite unconscious.'

'Ah, yes,' said the Doctor. 'Now I remember. And you were taken away again the following morning before I was up. I never got a chance to talk to you. How did you come to get so badly smashed up?'

'I was run over,' said the rat, a far-away look of reminiscence coming into his eyes, 'by a perambulator containing two heavy twins. It happened – well, it's a long story.'

'I'd like to hear it,' said the Doctor. 'After dinner is a good time for stories.'

'I would gladly tell it,' said the Hotel Rat, 'if the company has time for it.'

At once a little buzz of pleased expectant excitement ran through the big crowd as every one settled down to listen in comfort. There is nothing that rats and mice love more than stories, and something told them that this one would likely be interesting.

'It was about five years ago,' the Hotel Rat began, 'that I first started living in hotels. Some rats say they're dangerous places to make your home in. But I don't think, once you get used to them, they are any more unsafe than other places. And I love the changeful life you meet with there, folks coming and going all the time. Well, I and a couple of brothers of mine found a nice old hotel in a country town, not far from here, where the cooking was good, and we determined to settle down there. It had fine rambling big cellars; and there was always lots of food lying around, from the oats in the horses' stables across the yard to the scraps of cheese and bread on the dining-room floor. With us another rat came to live – a very peculiar character. He was not quite – er – respectable, as people call it. None of the ordinary rat colonies would let him live with them. But I happened to save his life from a dog once, and ever after that he followed me round. Leery, he was called. And he had only one eye.

'Leery was a wonderful runner. They said he cheated at the races. But I never quite believed that part of his bad reputation, because with a wind and a lightning speed like his, he didn't have to cheat – he could win everything easily without. Anyway, when he asked me if he could live with us I said to my older brother, "Snop," I said (my brothers' names were Snip and Snop), "I think there's a lot of good in Leery. You know how people are: once a rat gets a bad name they'll believe anything against him and

nothing for him. Poor Leery is an outcast. Let's take him in."

' "Well," said Snop, "I suppose it will mean that most of our friends will refuse to know us. And Leery certainly is a tough-looking customer. He's only got one eye, and that's shifty. Still, I don't care about society's opinions. If you want to have him to live with us, Snap" (that was my nickname in the family, Snap), "take him in by all means."

'So Leery became part of our household in the little old country-town hotel. And it was a very good thing for me he did, as you will see later on. Now there was one subject on which Leery and I never agreed. He was quite a philosopher, was Leery. And he always used to say, "Rely on yourself – on your wits. That's my motto." While I, I always pinned my faith to the protection of a good hole. You know there are an awful lot of dangers in an hotel – any number of dogs, two or three cats at least, plenty of traps and rat-poison, and a considerable crowd of people coming and going all the time. The hole I had made for myself (it joined up with those of my brothers, but it only had one door which we all used) was the nicest and snuggest I have ever been in. It was alongside the back of the kitchen chimney and the bricks were always warm from the fire. It was a wonderful place to sleep on winter nights.

' "Well, Leery," I would say, "myself, I always feel safe when I get back to the home hole. I don't care what happens so long as I'm in my own comfortable home."

'Then Leery would screw up his one shifty eye and blink at me.

' "Just because it's familiar to you," he said – "because you know everything in it and love everything there, that doesn't mean it's a safe place, or a protection, at all."

' "Well, I don't know, Leery," said I. "In a way it's like a friend, one who will help defend you."

' "Oh, fiddlesticks!" said he. "You've got to carry your defence with you. A good hole won't save you always. You've got to rely on yourself; that's my motto – Rely on your wits."

'Now there were two cats living at the hotel. Mostly they'd snooze before the parlour fire. They got fed twice a day. And of course we hotel rats knew their habits and their daily programme hour by hour. We weren't really afraid of them because they were lazy and overfed. But about once a month they'd decide to go on a rat and mouse hunt together. And they knew where our holes were just as well as we knew what their habits were.

'Well, one day the Devil got into those two cats, and

they went on a rat hunt that lasted for three days. We got word that they were out on the warpath from one of our scouts – we had scouts on duty day and night, of course we had to, with all those dogs and cats and people about. And from then on we took no chances on being caught too far from a hole of some sort. But my own policy, as I told you, had always been to count on reaching my own hole. I didn't trust any others – not since I dived into a strange hole one day to get away from a dog and found a weasel in it who nearly killed me. However, to go back: late in the afternoon, returning home, I ran into both the cats at once. One was standing guard over the hole and the other made straight for me. I kept my head. I had been chased lots of times before, but never by two cats at once. There was no hope of my getting into my hole, so I turned about and leapt clean through the open window into the street.'

The Hotel Rat paused a moment to cough politely behind his paw; while the whole of the enormous audience, who had experienced the thrill of similar pursuits themselves, leaned forward in intense expectation.

'I landed,' he said at length, with a grimace of painful recollection, 'right under the wheels of a baby-carriage. The rear wheel passed over my body; and I knew at once that I was pretty badly hurt. The nursemaid gave a scream – "Ugh! A rat!" – and fled with the carriage and babies and all. Then I expected the cats would descend on me and polish me off right away. I was powerless; my two back legs wouldn't work at all, and all I could do was to drag myself along by my front paws at about the speed of a tortoise.

'However, my luck wasn't entirely out. Before the cats had time to spring on me a dog, attracted by the commotion, arrived on the scene at full gallop. He didn't even notice me. But he chased those two cats down the street at forty miles an hour.

'But my plight was bad enough in all conscience. I didn't know what was wrong, only that I was in terrific pain. Inch by inch, expecting to be caught by some enemy any moment, I began to drag myself back towards the window. Luckily it was a sort of cellar window, on a level with the street. If it hadn't been, of course I could never have got through it. It was only about a yard away from the spot where I had been injured, but never shall I forget the long agony of that short journey.

'And all the time I kept saying to myself over and over, "The hole! Once I'm back there I'll be all right. I must reach the home hole before those cats return."'

14

LEERY, THE OUTCAST

'MORE dead than alive,' the Hotel Rat went on, 'I did finally reach my home hole, crawled to the bottom of it and collapsed in a faint.

'When I came to, Leery was bending over me.

'"Ah, Snap," said he with tears in his eyes, "this is one place where your philosophy doesn't work."

'"What's the matter with me?" I asked. "What's broken?"

'"Both your hind legs," said he. "We've got to get you to Doctor Dolittle, over to Puddleby. Your home hole is no help to you this time."

'My two brothers were there, Snip and Snop; and the three of them put their heads together to work out a way to get me to the Doctor's. They found an old slipper somewhere which they said would do for a stretcher or a sort of sleigh-ambulance. They were going to put me in it and drag it along the ground.'

'What, not all the way to Puddleby?' cried the Doctor.

'No,' said the Hotel Rat. 'They had done some scouting outside. All the rats in most of the colonies around had heard about the accident and had helped with their advice and in any other way they could. And a farm wagon had been found loaded with cabbages, standing in an inn yard down the street. It was going to Puddleby first thing in the morning. Their idea was to drag me to the yard in their shoe-ambulance, hide me among the cabbages, and at Puddleby watch their opportunity to get me across to your house.

'Well, everything was in readiness, and they had me tucked up in the ambulance, when Leery comes running

back from the mouth of the hole swearing something terrible.

'"We can't go yet," he whispered. "Those horrible cats have come back and they've mounted guard outside the hole. They know well enough we've only got one entrance. I nearly walked right into their paws just now. We're nicely trapped! Give me the open, town or country, any day."

'So, there was nothing to do but to wait. My legs were getting worse and worse all the time and I had an awful high fever. Leery annoyed me by keeping on talking about relying on yourself.

'"This shows you," says he: "What's the good of a

94

fine hole now? We want to get out of it and we can't. You've got to rely on your wits, on yourself. That's my motto."

'"Oh, be quiet!" I cried. "Such a comfort you are to have at a sick-bed! My head feels red-hot. Pour some cold water over it. You'll find a thimbleful over there in the corner."

'But if Leery's bedside manner was not as cheerful as it might be, still in the end he saved my life – and nearly lost his own in doing it. The best part of a day went by and those horrible cats still kept watch at the mouth of the hole. I was so bad now that I was only conscious in short spells – and even then sort of delirious with fever.

'In one of my clear moments, after Leery had been watching me for a few minutes he turned to my brothers and said:

'"There's only one thing to be done. Those cats may stick on at the mouth of the hole for another couple of days. Snap can't last much longer. If we can't get him to the Doctor soon, it's all up with him. He saved my life once, did Snap. Now's the time I can pay back the debt – or try to, I'm going to give those cats a run."

'"What," cried my brothers, "you mean to try and draw them off?"

'"Just that," said Leery, winking with his one shifty eye. "I'm the fastest rat in the country. If I can't do it, no one can. You pull the shoe up to the mouth of the hole and stand ready. In a little while it will be late enough so that the streets are nearly empty. I'll give them a run right round the town. Get Snap down to that inn-yard. There's a cart full of cabbage leaves there every morning just about daylight. If I'm lucky I can keep those two mean brutes busy till you've had time to get him in among the cabbages."

'"There are two cats, remember," said my brothers. "Look out! If you get caught we'll only be one less to get him to the Doctor's."

'Well, they drew my shoe-ambulance up to within about three inches of the mouth of the hole. Then Leery, one-eyed outcast, champion runner and faithful friend, went up to the entrance. The light of the street-lamps, coming in through the window, shone down into the hole and lit up his ugly face. You could see too the shadows of those beastly cats, waiting – waiting with the patience of the Devil.

'It was indeed a dramatic moment. Leery was a born gambler; I had often seen him bet all he had on any reckless chance, apparently for the fun of the thing. And so, I think, in his own strange way he rather enjoyed this theatrical situation.

'With a little wriggle of his hind quarters he made ready for the leap – the most daring leap of his life.

'Then, *zip*! – he was gone!

'Instantly we heard a scuffle as the two cats wrenched around and started off in pursuit.

'Then for a whole hour Leery played the most dangerous game a rat can play, hide-and-seek with two angry cats, touch-and-go with double death. First he led them down the street at full speed. He had his whole programme mapped out in his own mind, with every stop, trick, and turnabout. There was a little yard behind a house he knew of. In that yard there was a small duck-pond; and in the pond a cardboard box was floating. Leery led the chase into the yard, leapt the pond, using the box as a sort of stepping-stone. The cat who was farthest ahead followed him, but found out too late that the floating box would take a rat's weight but not a cat's. With a gurgle she went down out of sight and was kept busy for the rest of the night getting herself dry. She, for one, had had enough of hunting.

'But the other, realizing that she had a clever quarry to deal with, took no chances. She stuck to Leery like a leech – which was exactly what Leery wanted, so long as he could keep out of her clutches. He would slip into a hole just an inch ahead of her pounce. Then he'd get his breath while she waited, swearing, outside. And just as she was thinking of giving him up as a bad job and coming back to our hole after me, he'd pop out again and give her another run.

'All round the town he went: down into cellars; up on to roofs; along the tops of break-neck walls. He even led her up a tree, where she thought she'd surely get him in the

upper branches. But right at the top he took a flying leap across on to a clothes-line – from which he actually jeered at her and dared her to follow.

'In the meantime Snip and Snop were trundling me along the road in my shoe-ambulance. I never had such a dreadful ride. Twice they spilled me into the gutter. At last they reached the inn-yard and somehow got me up into the wagon and stowed me away among the cabbages. As daylight appeared the wagon started on its way. Oh dear, how ill I felt! Luckily that load of cabbages came into Puddleby by the Oxenthorpe Road. They dropped me off the tail of the cart right at the Doctor's door – only just in time to save my life. But without Leery the outcast it could never have been done. One of my brothers, Snip, hustled back at once to the hole and hung about for hours waiting for Leery, worried to death that he might have paid the price of his life to save mine. For both of them realized now that even if Leery was an outcast from Rat Society, he was a hero just the same. About eight o'clock in the morning he strolled in chewing a straw as though he had spent a pleasant day in the country. . . .

'Well, after all, I suppose he was right: in the end you have to rely on your wits, on yourself.'

15

THE VOLCANO RAT

THE adventure related by the Hotel Rat reminded various members of things of interest in their own lives – as is often the case with stories told to a large audience. And as soon as it was ended a buzz of general conversation and comment began.

'You know,' said the Doctor to the white mouse, 'you rats and mice really lead much more thrilling and exciting lives than we humans do.'

'Yes, I suppose that's true,' said the white mouse. 'Almost every one of the members here has had adventures of his own. The Volcano Rat, for instance, has a very unusual story which he told me a week or so ago.'

'I'd like to hear some more of these anecdotes of rat and mouse life,' said the Doctor. 'But I suppose we ought to be getting home now. It's pretty late.'

'Why don't you drop in again some other night – soon?' said the white mouse. 'There's always quite a crowd here in the evenings. I've been thinking it would be nice if you

or Tommy would write out a few of these life-stories of the members and make them into a book for us, a collection. We'd call it, say, "Tales of the Rat and Mouse Club."'

At this suggestion quite a number of rats and mice who had been listening to our conversation joined in with remarks. They were all anxious for the honour of having their own stories included in the club's book of adventures. And before we left that night it was agreed that we should return the following evening to hear the tale of the Volcano Rat. I knew it would be no easy matter for me to take down the stories word for word. But the white mouse said he would see that they were told slowly and distinctly; and with the Doctor's assistance (his knowledge of rat and mouse language was of course greatly superior to mine) I thought I might be able to manage it. I was most anxious to, for we both realized that by this means we would add a book of great distinction to Animal Literature.

Considerable excitement and rejoicing were shown when it became known that we had consented to the plan. It was at once arranged that a notice should be put up on the club bulletin-board, in the room called the Lounge, showing which member was chosen to tell his story for each night in the week. And as we carefully rose from our seats and made our difficult way down the tunnel into the open air, we heard rats and mice all round us assuring one another they would be certain to come tomorrow night.

When he arose amid a storm of applause the following evening to address the large audience gathered to hear his story, the Volcano Rat struck me at once by his distinctly foreign appearance. He was the same colour as most rats, neither larger nor smaller; but there was something Continental about him – almost Italian, one might say. He had sparkling eyes and very smooth movements, yet clearly he was no longer young. His manner was a rather curious mixture of gaiety and extreme worldliness.

'Our president,' he began with a graceful bow towards the white mouse, 'was speaking last night of the high state of civilization to which, through Doctor John Dolittle and our club, this community has reached. Tonight I would like to tell you of another occasion – perhaps the only other occasion in history – when our race rose to great heights of culture and refinement.

'Many years ago I lived on the side of a volcano. For all we knew, it was a dead volcano. On its slopes there were two or three villages and one town. I knew every inch of the whole mountain well. Once or twice I had explored the crater at the top – a great mysterious basin of sponge-

like rock, with enormous cracks in it running way down into the heart of the earth. In these, if you listened carefully, you could hear strange rumbling noises deep, deep down.

'The third occasion when I went up to the crater I was trying to get away from some farm dogs who had been following my scent through the vineyards and olive groves of the lower slopes. I stayed up there a whole night. The funny noises sort of worried me; they sounded so exactly like people groaning and crying. But in the morning I met an old, old rat who, it seemed, lived there regularly. He was a nice old chap and we got to chatting. He took me all round the crater and showed me the sights – grottoes, steaming underground lakes and lots of queer things. He lived in these cracks in the mountain.

'"How do you manage for food?" I asked.

'"Acorns," he replied. "There are oak trees a little way down the slope. And I lay in a good big store each autumn. And then for water there's a brook or two. I manage all right."

'"Why, you live like a squirrel!" I said – "storing up your nuts for the winter. What made you choose this place for a home?"

'"Well, you see," said he, "truth is, I'm getting old and feeble. Can't run like I used to. Any cat or dog could catch me in the towns. But they never come up here to the crater. Superstitious! They're afraid of the rumbling voices. They believe there are demons here."

'Well, I lived with the old Hermit Rat for two days. It was a nice change after the noisy bustling life of the town. It was a great place just to sit and think, that crater. In the evenings we would squat on the edge of it, looking down at the twinkling lights of the town far, far below – and the sea, a misty horizon in blue-black, far out beyond.

'I asked the old rat if he didn't often get lonely, living up there all alone.

'"Oh, sometimes," said he. "But to make up for the loneliness, I have peace. I could never get that down there."

'Every once in a while, when the rumbling voices coming out of the heart of the mountain got louder, he'd go down a crack and listen. And I asked him what it was he expected to hear. At first he wouldn't tell me and seemed afraid that I might laugh at him or something. But at last he told me.

'"I'm listening for an eruption," says he.

'"What on earth is that?" I asked.

'"That's when a volcano blows up," says he. "This one

has been quiet a long time, many years. But I've listened to those voices so long that I can understand 'em. – Yes, you needn't laugh," he added, noticing I was beginning to grin. "I tell you I've an idea that I shall know – for certain – when this mountain is going to blow up. The voices will tell me."

'Well, of course I thought he was crazy. And after I had grown tired of the lonely life myself, I bade him good-bye and came back to live in the town.

'It was not long after that that the citizens imported a whole lot of cats of a new kind. Us rats had got too plenti-ful and the townsfolk had made up their minds to drive us out. Well, they did. These cats were awful hunters. They never stopped; went after us day and night. And as there were thousands of them, life for us became pretty nearly impossible.

'After a good many of our people had been killed some of the leaders of the colonies got together in an old cellar one night to discuss what we should do about it. And after several had made suggestions which weren't worth much, I started thinking of my old friend the hermit and the peaceful life of his crater-home. And I suggested to the meeting that I should lead them all up there, where we could live undisturbed by cats or dogs. Some didn't like the idea much. But beggars can't be choosers. And it was finally decided that word should be passed round to all the rats in the town that at dawn the next day I would lead them forth beyond the walls and guide them to a new home.'

16

THE VOICES IN THE EARTH

'So,' the Volcano Rat continued, 'the following day a great departure of rats took place from that town. And the old hermit of the mountain-top had the surprise of his life when from his crow's-nest look-out he saw several thousand of us trailing up the slope to share his loneliness.

'Fortunately the autumn was not yet over and there were still great quantities of acorns lying beneath the oak trees. These we harvested into the many funny little underground chambers with which the walls of the crater were riddled.

'Because I had led them out of danger into this land of safety I came to be looked upon as a sort of leader. Of course after the first excitement of the migration was over

a good deal of grumbling began. It seems people always have to grumble. Many young fellows who thought themselves clever made speeches to those willing to listen. They told the crowd that I had led them into as bad a plight as they were in before. Rat and mouse civilization had gone backward, they said, instead of forward. Now they were no better than squirrels living on stored-up acorns. Whereas in the towns, though they may have had the constant dangers that always had to be faced in cities, life at least had some colour and variety; they hadn't got to eat the same food *every* day; and if they wanted to line their nests with silk or felt they knew where to find it, etc., etc., etc., and a whole lot more.

'These discontented orators got the common people so worked up against me that for a time my life was actually in danger from the mob. Finally – though I am a rat of few words – I had to make a speech on my own account in self-defence. I pointed out to the people that the life we were now leading was nothing more nor less than the original life of our forefathers. "After the Flood," I told them, "this was how you lived, the simple outdoor life of the fields. Then when the cities of Men arose with their abominable crowding you were tempted by the gay life of cellars and larders. We rats," I said proudly, "were at the first a hardy race of agriculturists, living by corn and the fruits of the earth. Lured by idleness and ease, we became a miserable lot of crumb-snatchers and cheese-stealers. I gave you the chance to return to your healthy, independent, outdoor life. Now, after you have listened to these wretched cellar-loungers, you long to go back to the sneaking servitude of the dwellings of Men. Go then, you fleas, you parasites!" (I was dreadfully cross.) "But never," I said, "never ask me to lead you again!"

'And yet Fate seemed to plot and conspire to make me a leader of rats. I didn't want to be. I never had any taste or ambition for politics. But no sooner had I ended my speech, even while the cheers and yells of the audience were still ringing in my ears (for I had completely won them over to my side), the old hermit came up behind me and croaked into my ear, "The eruption! – the voices in the earth have spoken. Beware! We must fly!"

'Something prompted me to believe him – though even to this day I don't see how he could have known, and I thought I had better act, and act quickly, while I had the crowd on my side.

' "Hark!" I shouted, springing to my feet once more. "This mountain is no longer safe. Its inner fires are about

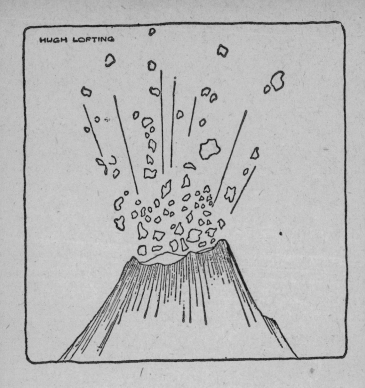

to burst forth. All must leave. Do not wait to take your acorns with you. For there is no time to lose."

'Then like one rat they rose up and shouted, "Lead us and we will follow. We believe in you. You are the leader whom we trust!"

'After that came a scene of the wildest kind. In a few minutes I had to organize a train of thousands of rats and mice and get it down that mountain-side the quickest possible way. Somehow or other I managed it – even though darkness came on before I started them off and the route was precipitous and dangerous. In addition to everything else, I had to make arrangements for six rats to carry the old hermit, who couldn't walk fast enough to keep up with the rest.

'So, through the night, past the walls of the town – the town which had turned us out – we hurried on and on and on, down, down into the valley. Even there, tired though we all were, I would not let them halt for long, but hurried the train on after a few moments' rest across the valley, over the wide river by a stone bridge and up the slopes of another range of hills twenty miles away from the spot we had started from. And even as I wearily shouted the command to halt, the volcano-top opened with a roar and sent a funnel of red fire and flying rocks hurtling into the black night sky.

'Never have I seen anything so terrifying as the anger of that death-spitting mountain. A sea of red-hot stones and molten mud flowed down the slopes, destroying all in its path. Even where we stood and watched, twenty miles away across the valley, a light shower of ashes and dust fell around us.

'The next day the fire had ceased and only a feather of smoke rising from the summit remained. But the villages were no more; the town, the town that had turned us out, could not be seen.

'Well, we settled down to country life and for some years lived in peace. My position as leader, whether I willed it or no, seemed more than ever confirmed now that I had led the people out of further dangers.

'And so time passed and the Second Migration was declared a great success. But presently, as always seemed to be the way, I foresaw that before long we would have to move again. Our trouble this time was weasels. Suddenly in great numbers they cropped up all over the countryside and made war on rats, mice, rabbits, and every living thing. I began to wonder where I would lead the people

this time. Often I had looked across the valley at our old mountain, our old home. The hermit had told me that he was sure that the volcano would not speak again for fifty years. He had been right once: he probably would be again. One day I made up my mind to go back across the valley and take a look around. Alone I set off.

'Dear me, how desolate! The beautiful slopes that had been covered with vineyards, olive groves and fig trees were now grey wastes of ashes, shadeless and hot in the glaring sun. Wearily I walked up the mountain till I came to about the place where I reckoned the town had stood. I began wondering what the buildings looked like underneath. I hunted around and finally found a hole in the lava;

through it I made my way downward. Everything of course, after all these years, was quite cold; and to get out of the sun into the shade beneath the surface of the ground was in itself a pleasure. I started off to do some subterranean exploring.

'Down and down I burrowed. In some places it was easy and in some places it was hard. But finally I got through all that covering of ashes and lava crust and came into the town beneath.

'I almost wept as I ran all over it. I knew every inch of the streets, every stone in the buildings. Nothing had changed. The dead city stood beneath the ground, silent and at peace, but in all else just as it had been when the rain of fire had blotted it out from the living world.

'"So!" I said aloud, "here I will bring the people – back to the town that turned us out. At last we have a city of our own!"'

17

THE UNITED RAT STATES
REPUBLIC

THE white mouse, seeing that the Volcano Rat seemed a little hoarse, motioned to a club waiter to fetch water – which was promptly done.

With a nod of thanks to the chairman the Volcano Rat took a sip from the acorn-cup and then proceeded.

'On my return I called the people together and told them that the time had come for our Third Migration. Many, when they found out whither I meant to lead them, grumbled as usual – this time that I was taking them back to the place from which we had already once taken flight.

' "Wait!" I said. "You complained years ago that I had set your civilization back, that I had reduced you to the level of squirrels. Well, now I'm going to give you a chance to advance your civilization to a point it never dreamed of before. Have patience."

'So, once more under the protection of darkness, I led the people across the valley and up the slopes of the sleeping mountain. When I had shown them where to dig, holes were made by the hundred, and through them we entered into possession of our subterranean town.

'It took us about a month to get the place in working order. Tons of ashes had to be removed from doorways, a great deal of cleaning up was needed, and many other things required attention. But it would take me more than a month to tell you in detail of the wonderful Rat City we made of it in the end. All the things which Men had used were now ours. We slept in feather beds. We had a marble swimming pool, built originally by the Romans, to bathe in. We had barbers' shops furnished with every imaginable perfume, pomade and hair-oil. Fashionable rat ladies went to the manicure establishments and beauty-parlours at least twice a week. And well-groomed dandies promenaded of an evening up and down the main street. We had athletic clubs where wrestling, swimming, boxing and jumping contests were held. All the best homes were filled with costly works of art. And an atmosphere of education and culture was everywhere noticeable.

'Of course much of the food which was in the town when the catastrophe happened had since decayed and become worthless. But there were great quantities of things that were not perishable, like corn, raisins, dried beans, and what not. These at the beginning were taken over by me and the Town Council as city property; and for the first month every rat who wanted an ounce of corn had

to work for it. In that way we got a tremendous lot of things done for the public good, such as cleaning up the streets, repairing the houses, carrying away rotting refuse, etc.

'But perhaps the most interesting part of our new city life was the development of professions and government. In our snug town beneath the earth we were never disturbed by enemies of any kind, except occasional sickness; and we grew and flourished. At the end of our first year of occupation a census was taken, and it showed our population as ten and three-quarter millions. So you see we were one of the largest cities in history. For such an enormous colony a proper system of government became very necessary. Quite early we decided to give up the municipal plan and formed ourselves into a city republic with departments and a Chamber of Deputies. Still later, when we outgrew that arrangement, we reorganized and called ourselves The United Rat States Republic. I had the honour of being elected the first Premier of the Union Parliament.

'After a while of course rats from outside colonies got to hear of our wonderful city, and tourists were to be seen on our streets almost any day in the week looking at the sights. But we were very particular about whom we took in as citizens. If you wanted citizenship you had to pass quite serious examinations both for education and for health. We were especially exacting on health. Our Medical College – which turned out exceptionally good rat doctors – had decided that most of our catching diseases had been brought in first by foreigners. So after a while a law was passed that not even tourists and sightseers could be admitted to the town without going through a careful medical examination. This, with the exceptionally good feeding conditions, the freedom of the life and the popular interest in sports and athletics, made the standard of physical development very high. I don't suppose that at any time in the whole history of our race have there been bigger or finer rats than the stalwart sons of the United Rat States Republic. Why, I've seen young fellows in our high-school athletic teams as big as rabbits and twice as strong.

'Building and architecture were brought to a very fine level, too. In order to keep the lava and ashes from falling in on us we constructed in many places regular roofs over the streets and squares. Some rats will always love a hole, even if you give them a palace to live in. And many of us clung to this form of dwelling still.

HUGH LOFTING

'One morning I was being measured for a new hole by a well-known digging contractor when my second valet rushed in excitedly waving the curling-irons with which he used to curl my whiskers.

'"Sir," he cried, "the Chief of the Street Cleaning Department is downstairs and wants to be admitted at once. Some Men have come. They are digging into the mountainside above our heads. The roof over the Market Square is falling in and the people are in a panic!"

'I hurried at once with the Chief of the Street Cleaning Department to the Market Square. There I found all in the greatest confusion. Men with pick-axes and shovels were knocking in the roof of lava and ashes which hid our city from the world. The moment I saw them I knew it was the end. Man had returned to reclaim the lost town and restore it to its former glory.

'Some of our people thought at first that the newcomers might only dig for a little while and then go away again. But not I. And sure enough, the following day still more Men came and put up temporary houses and tents and went on digging and digging. Many of our hot-headed young fellows were for declaring war. A volunteer army, calling itself *The Sons of Rat Freedom*, three million strong, raised itself at the street-corners overnight. A committee of officers from this army came to me the third day and pointed out that with such vast numbers they could easily drive these few Men off. But I said to them:

' "No. The town, before it was ours, belonged to Man. You might drive them off for a while; but they would come back stronger than ever, with cats and dogs and ferrets and poison; and in the end we would be vanquished and destroyed. No. Once more we must migrate, my people, and find ourselves new homes."

'I felt terribly sad, as you can easily imagine. While I was making my way back through the wrecked streets to my home, I saw some of the Men preparing to take away a statue of myself carved by one of our most famous rat sculptors. It had been set up over a fountain by the grateful townsfolk to commemorate what I had done for them. On the base was written, *"The Saviour of His People – The Greatest of All Leaders."* The men were peering at the writing, trying to decipher it. I suppose that later they put the statue into one of their museums as a Roman relic or something. It was a good work of art – even if the rat sculptor did make my stomach too large. Anyhow, as I watched them I determined that I would be a leader of rats no more. I had, as it were, reached the top rung of the

ladder; I had brought the people to a higher pitch of civilization than they had ever seen before. And now I would let some one else lead them. The Fourth Migration would be made without me.

'Sneaking quietly into my home I gathered a few things together in a cambric handkerchief. Then I slipped out and by unfrequented back streets made my way down the mountain-side – suddenly transformed from a Prime Minister of the biggest government, the greatest empire our race had ever seen, into a tramp-rat, a lonely vagabond.'

18

THE MUSEUM MOUSE

As the Volcano Rat ended his story there followed a queer little silence. That final picture of the great leader leaving the wonderful civilization he had built up and journeying forth alone rather saddened the audience. John Dolittle was the first to speak.

'But what became of the rest of your people?' he asked.

'I did not hear until much later,' the Volcano Rat replied. 'I took to the sea. I boarded a ship in the first harbour I came to and sailed away for foreign shores. A year or more afterwards I learned from some rats I met – when I was changing ships to come here – that several of the young wild volunteers had succeeded in getting the people to go to war. The results had been just about what I had prophesied. In the first battle between Men and Rats the rats had easily won and driven the enemy from the mountain-side. But a week later the Men came back armed with shotguns, smoke-pots, and other engines of war; and in their train came cats and dogs and ferrets. The slaughter of rats was apparently just horrible. Millions were wiped out. Panic seized the rest and a general mad flight followed. The slopes were simply grey with rats as the whole population left the underground city and ran for the valley. There were far too many for the dogs and cats to kill and so quite a few reached safety; but they were widely scattered. And no attempt was made to reorganize the remnant of a great race under another government. The United Rat States Republic was no more.'

The white mouse now arose from the presidential chair

and after thanking the Volcano Rat for his story reminded
the members that tomorrow night, Tuesday the fifteenth, the
Museum Mouse had promised to entertain them. The meeting was then declared adjourned and every one went home.

The next evening, in spite of the fact that both the
Doctor and I were very busy, we were in our places in the
Assembly Room by eight o'clock because we did not want
to miss the adventures of the Museum Mouse. We knew
him to be quite a personality. He had already interested us
considerably by his observations on natural history. He
looked something like a little old professor himself. He had
tiny beady black eyes and a funny screwed-up look to his
sharp-nosed face. His manner was cut and dried.

HUGH LOFTING

'I've lived all my life in natural history museums,' he began. 'Main reason why I like them is because when they're closed to the public you have the place to yourself – from six in the evening to ten o'clock the next morning, and till two in the afternoon on Sundays. This story is mainly concerned with the nest of the Three-ringed Yah-yah, a strange East Indian bird who builds a peculiar home; and with Professor Jeremiah Foozlebugg, one of the silliest animal-stuffers I ever knew.

'Why, just to show you how stupid that professor was: one day he was putting together the skeleton of a pre-historic beast, the Five-toed Pinkidoodle – '

'The *what*?' cried the Doctor, sitting up.

'Well, I was never good on names,' said the Museum Mouse. 'It was a five-toed something. Anyway, while he was out of the room a moment his dog dragged in an old ham-bone and left it among the parts of the skeleton. And would you believe it? Jeremiah Foozlebugg spent days and nights trying to fit that ham-bone into the skeleton of the five-toed – er – thimajigg and wondering why there was one bone left over.

'Now, when I was first married I took my wife for a wedding trip to the natural history museum. And after I had shown her all over it she thought she'd like to settle down there. And we began to look about to decide where in the building we would make our home.

'"It must be a snug, warm place, Nutmeg," says she, "on the children's account. It's a risky business raising young mice where there are draughts and cold winds."

'"All right, Sarsparilla," I said. "I know the very spot. Come with me."

'Now, what we called the Stuffing Room was a long workshop downstairs where Foozlebugg and his assistants stuffed birds and animals and prepared specimens of plants and butterflies and things to be brought up later and put in the glass cases for the public to look at. All natural history museums have more collections and specimens presented to them than they can possibly use. And our Stuffing Room was always littered up with everything from elephants' tusks to fleas in bottles. Among all this junk there was a collection of birds' nests – many of them with the limb of the tree in which they had been built. For months and months this collection had lain upon a dusty shelf – nests of all sizes, shapes and sorts. One was quite peculiar. It was the nest of the Three-ringed Yah-yah. In form it was quite round, like a ball, and had for entrance one little hole – just big enough for a mouse to slip through.

When you were inside no one would know you were there.

'I showed it to Sarsparilla and she was delighted. Without further delay we got some extra scraps of silk, which Foozlebugg had been using for some of his stuffing business, and lined it soft and snug – although it was already well padded with horsehair and thistledown by the Three-ringed Yah-yah who had built it. Then for several days we led a peaceful happy life in our new home. During regular hours in the workshop we lay low and often had hard work stopping our giggles as we watched Professor Foozlebugg stuffing animals all out of shape and calling on his assistants to admire them.

'Well, the children came and then we were very glad about our selection of a home. For no place could have been more ideal for baby mice than was that old bird's nest with its round walls and draught-proof ceiling and floor. Now, there is one disadvantage in living in museums: you have to go out for all your meals. There's practically nothing to eat in the building, and what there is, like waxes and things of that sort, you soon learn to leave strictly alone, because those old professors use strong poisons on all their stuffing materials to keep the moth from getting into them. Of course even with all the doors locked any mouse can find his way in and out of a building somewhere. But occasionally, when the weather is bad, it is very inconvenient to have to go out for every single thing you eat. And now with a family of youngsters to feed this problem became more serious than usual.

'So Sarsparilla and I used to take it in turns to look after the youngsters while the other went out foraging for food. Sometimes we had to go a long way and to bring crumbs from various places to the lobby of the building before we hauled them down to the Stuffing Room. Well, one night I had been up very late foraging for food and didn't get in

HUGH LOFTING

until nearly daylight. I was dog-tired, but even then I didn't get any sleep because the children were querulous and fretful and they kept me awake. As soon as evening came Sarsparilla left me in charge and started out on her food hunt. Shortly after she had gone the children settled down quietly, and right away, worn out with fatigue, I fell into a deep sleep.

'When I awoke the sunlight was streaming in through the entrance-hole of our nest. I supposed I must have long over-slept. But I never remembered the direct rays of the sun to have shone in at our door like this before. I got up and peeped out cautiously.

'I could hardly believe my eyes. *Our nest was no longer*

in the Stuffing Room! Instead, we were in a glass case in one of the main halls of the museum. Around us, on various twigs and stands and things, were the other nests of the old collection which had lain so long on the dusty shelf. Our house had been put on show for the public, shut up tight in a glass case; and that stupid old duffer Foozlebugg who had put it there was still standing outside, displaying his handiwork with great pride to a fat woman and two children who were visiting the museum!'

19

PROFESSOR FOOZLEBUGG'S MASTERPIECE

'WELL,' sighed the Museum Mouse, 'you can imagine how I felt. There I was with a whole family of youngsters, shut up in a glass case. I dare not show myself outside the nest, hardly, because, even when that ridiculous Professor Foozlebugg had moved away with the fat woman, odd visitors in ones and twos were always browsing by and looking in. It would be difficult to think of a more uncomfortable unprivate home than ours had become.

'However, there were moments when that end of the hall was free from visitors and attendants. And during one of these I suddenly saw Sarsparilla with a wild look in her eye frantically hunting about outside for her lost family. Standing at the door of the nest, I waved and made signs to her and finally caught her attention. She rushed up to the glass and called through it:

' "Get the children out of there, Nutmeg. Get them out at once!"

'That was the last straw.

' "Sarsparilla," I called back, "don't be a fool. Do you think I brought the nest and the children here myself? How am I to get them out? I can't bite through glass."

' "But they must be fed!" she wailed. "It is long past their morning meal-time."

' "Bother their morning meal-time!" said I. "What about my morning meal-time? They'll have to wait. We can't do anything till the museum closes to the public – at five o'clock. You had better get away from there before you get seen."

'But Sarsparilla, like all women, was quite unreasonable. She just kept running up and down outside the glass, moaning and wringing her hands.

' "Can't you give them some of that stuffed duck there, on the shelf above your head?" she moaned.

' "I could *not*," I said. "Stuffed museum duck is full of arsenic. Don't worry. They can manage until five – the same as me."

'Sarsparilla would have gone on arguing all day, I believe, if an attendant hadn't come strolling down to that end of the wing and made it necessary for her to hide.

'The rest of the day I had my hands full. For the children, having missed two meals, suddenly got as lively as crickets. They were all for climbing out of the nest – though they hadn't had their eyes open more than a few days. I could have slapped them.

' "Where's Ma?" they kept on saying. "What's happened to Ma? I'm hungry. Where's Ma? Let's go and find her."

'I tell you they had me busy, dragging them down from the hole one after another. *They* didn't care how many people were looking in the glass case. All that they cared about was that they were hungry and wanted Ma – the stupid little things!

'Never was I so glad in all my experience of museum routine to see the attendants clearing the people out of the halls and locking up the doors. I knew all those old fellows in uniform well. It was a funny life they led – generally pleasant enough. One of the things they had to do was to look out for bomb-throwers. Why people should want to throw bombs or set infernal machines in museums, of all places, I don't know. But they do – or, at all events, it is always expected that they will. That's why the attendants won't allow visitors to bring in parcels: they are afraid they may contain dynamite.

'One of these old men regularly brought his lunch with him and ate it behind the stuffed elephant when nobody was looking – he wasn't supposed to, you see. And the

few crumbs he left upon the floor were the only food that I ever managed to get *inside* the museum. As he changed his coat this evening some crusts fell out of the paper in which his bread and cheese had been wrapped. I knew that if I didn't get them that night the charwoman would sweep them up in the morning. But while I was still gazing at them hungrily out of my glass prison Sarsparilla came and collected them and brought them over to the case.

' "Nutmeg, I want to get these in to the children," she said.

' "Oh, for Heaven's sake, have some sense!" I snapped back. "The first thing we've got to do is to find a way in – or rather a way out."

'"Gnaw a hole through the floor," said she – "quite simple. You needn't be afraid of anyone seeing you now. The night watchman won't be stirring for another hour yet."

'"Don't you know," I said wearily, "that all these cases are zinc-lined? I can't bite through zinc any more than I can through glass."

'That started her off again. She threw up her hands.

'"Why, the children will starve to death!" she cried. And she recommenced her running backwards and forwards like a crazy thing.

'I saw I wasn't going to get any helpful ideas from her, so I began to look over the situation myself with an eye to working something out. First, I climbed all around the whole case, carefully inspecting the joints in the walls, the floor and the roof, to see if I could find a weak spot anywhere. Then I examined each shelf in turn to see if by chance I might come upon anything that could help me. And finally on the top shelf I discovered something that suggested a plan of escape.

'It was this: among the collection of birds' nests there were some of sea-birds. These were set among stones, just as certain gulls and such build – just a rough hollow of twigs and seaweed laid on the shingle of the beach. Here Professor Foozlebugg had quite surpassed himself in the art of tastefully displaying specimens. He had the whole top shelf set out like a scene on a lonely island where sea-birds would build. At the back there was a picture of the sea painted, with lighthouses and sailing ships and everything. And in front of this there were several stuffed birds and nests set among the stones of the beach. The stones were mostly round, of all sizes. And it occurred to me that I might very easily roll some of the larger ones off the top shelf. Then, if they struck something slanting

when they reached the bottom of the case, they would fly against the glass wall and break it.

'I wasted no time in getting to work. It was necessary to prepare a bouncing place where the stone would fall if my plan was to be a success. I slid down to the bottom of the case and gathered together a large pile of stiff twigs which I took from the other nests. It was hard work, because most birds put their nests together pretty firmly. I made a frightful mess of the collection before I was done.

'In the meantime, not being able to keep the children in order while I was at work, I had let them follow their own sweet wills. Every one of the little beggars had got out of the nest; and now having seen "Ma" outside the case, they too were running up and down alongside the glass and careering all over the place trying to find a way out. If Professor Foozlebugg had come in at that moment to inspect his latest work of art he would have had a great shock.

'Well, when all was ready I went down below and chased all the children up on to the upper shelves so they wouldn't get hurt by falling stones or flying glass. Then I explained to Sarsparilla, in shouts, what I was going to do.

'"Stand by," I yelled, "to get the youngsters to a place of safety. They're not easy to handle."

'"All right," she called back. "I'll take three and you take three. And for pity's sake be careful how you get them through the hole in the broken glass."

'Then, just as I was about to put my shoulder under the round stone and topple it down, there came another shout from my wife:

'"Look out! – Night watchman coming! – Hide the children, quick!"

'It was all very well for Sarsparilla to say, "Hide the children, quick!" They had no intention of being hidden. They had seen "Ma" and they meant to get to her as soon as possible. And as soon as she disappeared again they went entirely crazy, rushing all over the place crying, "Where's Ma gone? We're hungry. What's become of Ma?"

'Oh dear! I never had such a time! I had no sooner caught a couple of them and hidden them behind a stuffed bird or something, before they would pop out again while I was running after the next pair.

'Luckily the night watchman was not a very wide-awake old man at the best of times, and as it happened tonight he did not swing his lantern near our case.

'When he had gone Sarsparilla appeared again outside the glass and I got ready to try my plan once more.

'*Crash!*

'It worked all right and no mistake. The stone knocked a hole in the front of the case big enough for a bulldog to get through. In fact everything would have gone splendidly if it hadn't been for those half-witted children of mine. With the crashing of the glass they just ran about like lunatics and we couldn't catch a single one of them. We had time to get away easily. But while we were still falling all over the place trying to get the family together, alarm bells in every corridor of the museum started ringing violently. The next thing, the night watchman came running through the hall shouting:

' "A bomb, a bomb! – Hey! Help! – Fire! Police! – A bomb's gone off somewhere! HELP!"

' "It's no use, Sarsparilla," I said. "We can't manage it now. Bring in one of those crusts of bread with you and come inside until the excitement dies down. Was anyone ever blessed with such children? Help me get them into the nest, quick! With you here, they'll be quieter and more manageable. Later, if luck is still with us, we may get away."

'And we only just got those little nuisances stowed out of sight in time. In less than five minutes from the crash of the glass people began arriving on the run. First, a policeman with a notebook from the beat outside the museum's main entrance. Then six firemen came rushing in dragging a hose. Next, the watchman's wife carrying bandages and a bottle of brandy.

'And all of them stood around the broken glass case asking about the "bomb". Yes, the watchman was quite sure it was a bomb. Look how it had wrecked all the nests inside!

'Then they gave their opinions, one after another: "Russian nihilists"; "suffragettes"; "East End anarchists", etc., etc. While all the time we, who were responsible for the whole thing, sat inside the home of the Three-ringed Yah-yah and listened to their silly chatter.

'Finally the great Professor Foozlebugg arrived on the scene, summoned from his bed – for it was now nearly midnight – by a messenger from the watchman. He nearly wept when he saw his latest work of art – his masterpiece – knocked all to pieces. He was much more upset about his beautiful scene on the seashore than he was over the museum's narrow escape from being blown up by an in-

fernal machine. He was about to wade into the wreckage then and there and put it to rights, but – fortunately for us – one of the policemen warned him off.

'"Don't touch it, sir, please. With these infernal machines, one never knows. A second, and more serious, explosion, sir, is liable to follow the moment you lay a finger on it. We will get the bomb experts from Police Head-quarters. They know how to handle these things, sir."

'Well, just that saved us from a pretty serious situation. After a little more discussion between the firemen and the constable it was decided to let well alone until the morning – when the bomb experts from Police Head-quarters would take charge of affairs. Meanwhile the policeman, the firemen and the professor felt they might as well go back to bed. As for the old watchman, he was so scared of that second explosion that the policeman had spoken of, that the moment the rest of them had departed he locked up the doors and left that hall severely to itself.

'Which, of course, was exactly what we wanted. We had seven peaceful hours before us – before the charwoman would come to sweep – in which to do our moving. The first thing we did, after we had all the children safely lifted out through the broken glass, was to sit down in the middle of the hall and eat a hearty meal off the crusts which the old attendant had left behind. Then we herded the children down below by easy stages to the Stuffing Room. And there Sarsparilla kept them together while I hunted up a new home among the lumber and stuff with which the shelves were littered.

'But this time, you may be sure, I did *not* pick a bird's nest, nor anything else that was likely to get put on exhibition while we slept.'

20

THE PRISON RAT

'I WOULD like very much to know,' said John Dolittle the following night when the Prison Rat was about to begin his story, 'what made you take to living in prisons. I've been in prison myself. And while I always found the life very quiet and restful, I would not recommend a jail as exactly a cheerful place to make one's permanent home.'

'Well,' the Prison Rat began, 'as a matter of fact, the story I am going to tell you explains how I took to prison life.'

'Good!' said the Doctor. And every one settled down to listen.

'To begin with, then,' said the Prison Rat, 'you must know that I began life as a studio rat. I patronized artists' studios. They're not bad places to live in. For one thing, artists, as a rule, are not very particular people; and a rat more or less doesn't bother them. And secondly, they always cook their own meals, and very seldom wash the dishes – after the meals; when they do, they do it before meals. Consequently there is always lots to eat. In almost any artist's studio you can be sure of finding a fish-head, or a chop-bone, or a plate with gravy stuck to the bottom, if you only hunt long enough.

'Well, then, after I had lived in several artists' studios and got sort of fond of the Bohemian life, I came to reside in one where the artist was rather peculiar. He lived all alone and seemed neither to have many friends nor to put himself out to make any. This was unusual. At my other studios they had parties – often – with lots of gaiety, laughter and good company. But this man hardly ever saw anyone. I think, maybe, he had been disappointed in love. But of that I am not sure. One old philosopher used to come and see him occasionally and they'd sit and talk and argue over politics far into the night.

'I never bothered about listening to them much; but one evening I overheard a word that made me stop behind the coal-scuttle with ears cocked. With practice I had become pretty good at understanding Man Talk – especially certain words that were repeated quite often.

' "Michael," – that was the artist's name – "why don't you get a cat?" asked the philosopher.

' "How absurd! What on earth would I get a cat for?" answered the other.

'You can be sure I was glad to hear him say that.

' "Well, a dog then – or something," the philosopher went on. "You're too lonely here altogether. It isn't good for you."

' "Oh, no," said the artist with a sort of far-away look in his eyes. "I don't need company. I can manage . . . alone."

'And then followed a very interesting discussion. It seemed that the artist was more of a philosopher than was the philosopher himself.

' "Why should I get a cat?" he repeated – "or a dog, or a goldfish, or a canary – or a wife? I tell you" – he leaned over and tapped the philosopher on the knee – "if you have attachments you are not free. I am alone. If I want to go away, I can go. If I had a family or a house full of pets, I could not."

'The philosopher finally was bound to agree with him. But just the same, I knew he was lonely, all by himself in that studio, in spite of his arguments. And the way I found it out was this: one day I slipped while I was hunting round the dishes and things for food and fell into a pail alongside the sink. The pail had no water in it; and ordinarily I could have leapt out again easily. But somehow I caught my leg as I fell and sprained it badly, and I couldn't jump an inch. And of course climbing out up the slippery sides was also quite impossible. I was trapped.

'Some time later the artist comes along, wanting the pail to carry water in. He looks into it and sees me. Of course I thought the end had come. You know how most people are: they all seem to think there is something virtuous about killing rats. And I'm pretty sure that even into his mind that was the first thought that came. Because he went off to the stove and came back with the poker. He looked determined and terrible enough. But suddenly his expression changed.

' "Oh, well," he muttered, "I suppose your life means something to you. Why should I kill you after all? ... Get out of my pail. I want to wash."

'And he deliberately rolled the pail over on to its side so I could escape. I limped off, thanking my lucky stars. I made a kind of slow progress with my sprained leg; and he watched me thoughtfully as I scrambled for a hole under the sink.

' "Humph! Had an accident?" he murmured. "Here, take this with you for supper."

'And he threw me a bacon-rind off the draining-board. I took it and tried to look gratefully at him before I disappeared into the hole.

'Then for several days after that he used to watch for me. And when I appeared, instead of flinging a boot at me, as most people do to rats, he used to throw crumbs of bread and meat. He was trying to make my acquaintance.

'That's how I knew that he was lonely.

'Another thing by which I was made still surer of it was that he used to talk to me a good deal – for want of some one else to chat with – also that he talked to himself a good deal. After a while I got quite tame; and as soon as I realized he didn't mind me knocking about the place quite freely, I used to sit up on a stool beside him and watch him paint. And I took my meals with him, too. He gave me an upturned bucket to sit on and seemed really interested in

what I liked to eat. He always called me Macchiavelli. I
never understood why. Perhaps that was a friend of his.

'"Macchiavelli," he would say, "you're the right kind of a
friend to have. You don't affect my liberty. If I leave the
studio I don't have to bother about you. You'll look after
yourself. Here's your good health, Macchiavelli – my friend
who leaves me free."

'And he would drink to me, with a bow, out of his shav-
ing-mug filled with beer.

'Now there were two or three other rats who lived under
the floor of that studio. And one day in spring three of us
went off together for a day's jaunt – just for a sort of
exploring trip, the way folks do in spring-time. As luck

would have it, a terrier picked up our trail and we got separated. The dog stuck to me finally, leaving the others alone. And he chased me a long way from home before I shook him off.

'I didn't get back to the studio until three days later. To my astonishment, I found that the artist was gone. The other rats had never been as tame with him as I was. They didn't trust Humans, they said, considering them a low-down, cruel and deceitful race, not in any way to be compared with rats for frankness and honesty. I asked them when and where the artist had gone. All that they could tell me was that some policemen had come and taken him away. They didn't understand Man Talk – at least, not as well as I did. But they had got the impression that it was something to do with a revolution in which the artist had taken part.

'Well, I cannot tell you how I felt. He had said that I was the right kind of a friend to have; that if he went away – it almost seemed as though he had foreseen it – it wouldn't make any difference to me. But it did. I positively wept as I went through the empty studio looking at his paintings. They were good pictures, too. And I made up my mind that I would find him if I had to seek through all the prisons in the land.

'And that was how I began my career as a prison rat.'

21

A RAT'S PILGRIMAGE

'WELL, my search indeed took me to strange places and brought me into touch with queer folk. I suppose I must have visited a good two dozen jails in all. I got to know a lot of prisoners, all kinds; political prisoners, as they were called, that is, people who had quarrelled with the Government; pick-pockets; coiners, makers of bad money; dog thieves; card sharps; men who had killed their fellow-men. It was quite interesting in a way – though most of it was very sad.

'They were all – or nearly all – anxious to make my acquaintance. And that was the first time that I discovered that, generally speaking, it is only in prison Men want to make friends of rats. Rather strange. I suppose it is because they are lonely and miserable in prison. All other places those same men would throw a brick at a rat, make a wry face and say, "Ooh! The brute!" But in prison they would make a friend of him – yes, in prison, where they have no friends. My artist, on the other hand, had been kind to me when he was free. That was the difference, to my way of thinking, between him and other people. And I made up my mind harder than ever to keep on hunting till I found him.

'Of course in my wanderings I also made the acquaintance of many other regular prison rats. And them I questioned always, hoping they might be able to give me some clue as to where my man had been taken. Some of them thought I was a fool to keep on searching for him.

' "Oh," they said, "he has forgotten about you long ago. Like as not, he won't know you when he sees you. If he wanted to make pets of rats there are always lots of them in every prison. And, anyway, never trust a man. Men are the sworn enemies of rats."

'But all I answered was, "He is in trouble and I want to find him. He was kind to me once – when *I* was in difficulties. Such things I don't forget."

'One of the prison rats I met suggested I go back to the studio and wait till some one came who might be con-

141

nected with the man I was seeking. Then by tracking him when he left, I might be led to the prison where the artist had been taken. I thought the idea was a good one and I acted on it. I went back to my old home and waited. About a week later the philosopher called. I watched him like a cat. He gathered some things together – clothes and books – wrapped them in a bundle and started away on foot.

'I followed. Luckily it was evening and the darkness gave me some chance of keeping in touch without being seen. It isn't so hard for a dog to follow a man through a town; but it is a very different matter for a rat.

'Well, in spite of several cats who tried to chase me off the trail I stuck to the old philosopher for a full half-hour.

HUGH LOFTING

'And then good luck deserted me – and him, too, poor fellow. He was run over at a street corner – a frightened horse. It was all done and finished so quickly there was hardly any telling how it happened. At first I thought the old man was killed. But he wasn't. Nevertheless he was badly enough hurt to make it necessary to call an ambulance and take him off to a hospital.

'So there went that hope. As I crouched in the shadow of a doorway and watched them taking him away, I realized with a sinking heart that not only was I losing my one clue, but my friend, the artist, was also losing the only other being in the world who would be likely to help him.

'Just the same, I set off on my hunt once more, more determined on this account than ever that I would find him – if I spent the rest of my life in doing it.

'Then for many weeks my pilgrimage continued without anything of importance happening. I went patiently from jail to jail, only staying in each one long enough to make sure that he wasn't there. After a while I got to do it more quickly than I had at the beginning. But it wasn't easy. You see, in most jails there were a great number of cells; and the first thing I did when I came to a new prison was to find out how many cells there were and how many of them were occupied. Then I had to discover some way of getting into each one in turn. If I couldn't get in – some of the newer jails were pretty hard even for a rat to get in or out of – I had to hang about somewhere till the prisoner was brought out for exercise so that I could get a look at his face. And, because in some cases the prisoners were brought out very seldom, this took a long time.

'Well, after two or three months I began to get somewhat discouraged, I must admit. However, I did not give up hope. Something told me, in spite of what the rats had said, that I was going to find him and that I was going to be of help to him.

'Now, there was a certain tune he had been in the habit of whistling in the studio when at work. And one day I had come to a new jail and looked at the prisoners in all the cells – all but one. This I couldn't find a way into, and the prisoner never seemed to get brought out. For nearly a week I had hung around that jail for the sake of that one cell alone, hoping a chance would come for me to see who was in there.

'At the end of the week I began seriously thinking of moving on to the next jail. After all it did not seem worth while for me to stay so long in one prison just on account of a single cell, when there were so many other jails yet to be visited. Still, I didn't quite like to go until I had made sure.

'And I'm glad I didn't. For that same night, as I hung about on watch outside the door, I heard – at last – the familiar whistle, his favourite tune. After nearly three months' search I had run him down! My word, didn't I feel pleased and proud!

'I set to work now with a lighter heart to the business of getting into that cell. So anxious was I to see him, that I took a fearful big chance. I decided to try and slip in with the warder who brought him his breakfast in the morning. This was pretty risky, because, as some of you may know, prison cells have precious little furniture that a rat can hide behind.

'Nevertheless I managed it. I stood ready in the shadow outside the door, and when the warder came along with the breakfast I slid in close behind his heels without being noticed. Then choosing the right moment, just as he was laying down the food, I nipped across under the prison cot and waited till he went out again, locking the door behind him. Then I came boldly forth from my hiding-place and showed myself.

' "Hullo!" said the artist. "Why, you look cheeky and brazen enough to be my friend Macchiavelli!"

'And then:

' "By George!" he added in a curious whisper. "It *is* Macchiavelli! I know him by that limp!"

'He looked thin and pale. But he seemed just as philosophical and just as ready to say funny, crazy, unexpected things as ever. He was really overjoyed to see me. He picked me up and patted me like a pet poodle.

' "My first visitor!" he kept saying – "My only visitor, in fact. Macchiavelli! – Good old Mack!"

'He invited me to share his breakfast with him, making apologies for the poorness of the fare.

'But the first thing I wanted to do, now that I knew where he was, was to find a way by which I could come in and go out of that cell with more or less safety. I looked around the walls and the floor, but there was no trace of a hole anywhere – and no chance of making any in the new, well-cemented stonework. Then I looked up at the little window, high in the wall. And that gave me an idea.

'I felt pretty sure that I could gain the sill of this window by scrambling up the rough stonework inside. I tried it. He stood below watching me climb, really terrified that I might fall and break my neck. From the sill I found that

the window could also be reached from the outside by means of a rain-water pipe which ran down the building near it.

'As soon as I got out I hunted up one of the rats who lived in the jail and questioned him. Also – I have told you that I was pretty good at understanding Man Talk – I listened at every opportunity I got to the conversations of the warders and attendants. And from what I could gather I came to the conclusion that my friend was soon to be transported, that is, sent away to serve a long term of imprisonment and labour in foreign parts. Exactly when he was to be taken I could not find out for certain. But I had a feeling that it was to be soon and that there was no time to lose.

'The next thing was to find out what my friend needed for escape. I consulted a very old rat who had lived in prisons all his life and seen several men escape. And he told me that the most important thing was a file to saw window-bars with. So a file, I determined, my man should have without delay. Now, the jail had a workshop in it where some of the prisoners were set to making things. But the men were always examined before they left the workshop to make sure they took no tools away to their cells. It didn't take me long to find my way into that workshop and pick out a nice sharp file – a small one that I could easily carry.

'In the middle of the night I revisited my friend – entering by way of the rain-water pipe and the window – and found him asleep. I woke him up by laying the file on his nose. At first he didn't know what to make of it. But when he realized what the piece of cold metal was that I had laid on his face he got up and set quietly to work at once.

'Well, that's about the end of my story. It took him two nights to cut through the bar; and I had to bring him a fresh file to replace the old one which was worn smooth. He got out of the window about midnight on the second night. No one saw him leave. Luck was with him and the sentry at the outside wall was kind of drowsy. He got clean away and left the country before they found him. I never saw him again. My assistance had only just got there in time, though. For when they came in on the third morning and found his cell empty, the prison van was already drawn up outside the gates of the jail waiting to take him to the ship.'

22

THE STABLE MOUSE

M Y book, entitled *Tales of The Rat and Mouse Club*, was by now beginning to look somewhat thick and bulky. Of course rewritten, or rather printed, as it would be in the bound volume itself, it would not take up as much space as it did in my rough copy. Nevertheless I could see by the end of the fourth story (that of the Prison Rat) that only about one more could be included in the book. I told this to the white mouse.

'Well,' said he, 'of course I see that you can't make the book too thick, otherwise it would be too heavy for the mouse readers to handle – and the rats have most of the volumes in the club library as it is. But there will be a terrible lot of disappointment. There are no less than nine members still hoping that their stories will be included – and I thought myself that you'd be able to get in another two, anyway.'

'Who are the members whose stories are still to be heard?' asked the Doctor.

'Oh, heavens, there's hundreds – hoping!' said the white mouse. 'But there are nine whom I had sort of half promised they would stand a chance. Out of that nine we shall now have to pick one – and of course there will be hard feelings. Let me see: there's the Railway Rat. His is a story of travel. Then – another voyager – the Ship's Rat, our old friend of the Canary Islands, Doctor. And there's the Icebox Mouse and the Theatre Mouse. I don't know much about them – new-comers to the club. Then there's the Zoo Rat, the chap who is always boasting of his acquaintance with the lion – and Cheapside says he does really go

in and out of his den. Next? – Let me think. . . . Oh, the
Tea-house Mouse. He is a sort of a tittering nincompoop.
A regular gossip, giggles all the time. It is easy to see how
and why he chose tea-houses to live in. I don't suppose his
story is much. Scandal, most likely. I should be glad to
cross him off the list. The Church Mouse, too, we can count
him out. His story will be a sort of a lecture, full of quota-
tions and advice to young mice. And I'm *so* tired of hearing
how poor he is. That leaves the Hansom-cab Mouse – his
yarn will be good, I suspect. . . . And the Hospital Mouse. I
tell you what I'll do: I'll get them all to give me a rough
outline of their stories and I'll pick the one which I think
is the best and relate it at the club tomorrow night, eh ?'

'All right,' said the Doctor. 'And you can tell the others that maybe there will be a second volume of *The Tales of the Rat and Mouse Club* – later – which they can all be in.'

To our surprise, when the Doctor and I took our places in the Assembly Room of the Rat and Mouse Club the following evening, we found that none of the members whom the President had spoken of last night had been selected to tell the fifth story for the book. Instead, a mouse whom neither of us had seen or heard of before got up and was introduced as the Stable Mouse.

'Her story was rather different, I thought,' the white mouse whispered in my ear. 'We want variety in the book. And those others were all jealous of one another. So I decided I'd take a new member altogether.'

The Stable Mouse was a quiet, lady-like little individual – rather shy. And at the beginning she had to be asked several times to speak louder, because some of the members at the back of the hall (a few of the old-age pensioners who lived in the club) could not hear her.

'This story is mostly about my first husband, Corky,' she began, 'a good-natured mouse, but the most frivolous-minded mate that anybody was ever asked to live with. It was largely on Corky's account that I became a stable mouse – thinking it was a safer place for him, one where he would be less likely to get into mischief and hot water. Stables are generally very good places for mice to live. There are always oats, which after all form the most nourishing and digestible food that can be found anywhere. And it is pleasant in the evenings when the horses come home from their work to sit up in the rafters and listen to them gossip about the day's doings.

'But even in a stable that husband of mine could find plenty of occasions to get himself into trouble and to keep

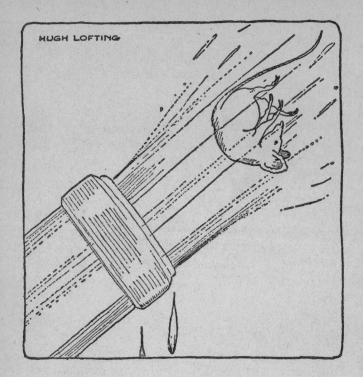

me worried to death. One day he found a large watering hose in a corner of the stable. And he thought it would be great fun to get into it and run up and down inside, as though it were a tunnel – sort of switchback idea. He was a regular child – I see that now: he never really grew up. Well, while he was playing this game, sliding and whooping round the loops of the hose, one of the stable-boys came and turned the water on to wash the stable floor. And of course, with the terrific force of the water, my husband was shot out of the hose like a bullet from a gun. His switchback gave him a much bigger ride than he expected. As it happened, the stable-boy had the hose pointed out in-to the yard when the water first rushed forth. And I suddenly saw Corky, gasping and half-drowned, flying over the pig-house roof. He landed in the pigs' trough on the other side – and very nearly got eaten by a large hog who mistook him for a floating turnip before he scrambled out to safety.

'Often I used to think that that light-headed husband of mine used to deliberately get himself into hot water – just for sheer devilment. And no amount of hard lessons seemed to teach him any sense. How it was that he wasn't killed in the first year of his life I don't know.

'Would you believe it? Time after time he used to get into the horses' nose-bags to steal their oats while they were actually eating! I told him often that one of these days he would get chewed up. What usually happened was that his moving around in the bags would tickle the horses' noses until they sneezed and blew him out on to the floor like a piece of chaff.

'One day this happened when the farmer who owned the place was standing in the stable with his wife. But this time the horse sneezed so hard that Corky was shot right up, nearly to the rafters. And when he came down he landed on the farmer's hat. The farmer thought it was just a drop of water leaking from the roof – it was raining at the time – and didn't take any notice. But presently, while his wife was talking to him, she suddenly saw Corky's nose peering over the brim of her husband's hat – wondering how he was going to get down to solid ground. Being, like most women, terrified of mice, she just lost her head, screamed and struck at Corky with her umbrella. She didn't hit him, but she nearly brained her husband – who, of course, thought that she had suddenly gone crazy. And in the general excitement that followed Corky, as usual, got away.

'But one day he had a very narrow escape, and if I hadn't been there to come to his assistance it would certainly have

been the end of his adventurous career. Now, there was an old jackdaw who used to hang about that stable-yard. Corky took a dislike to him from the start. And I am bound to say that he certainly was a churlish, grouchy curmudgeon of a bird. He used to watch from the stable roof, and if the farmer's wife threw out any nice titbits of food he would be down on them before we ever got a chance to start out for them. If we did get there first he would drive us off savagely with that great scissors-like bill of his. It didn't matter how much food there was, he wouldn't let us get any. The largest rats were scared of him, for he was worse than a game-cock to fight with. Even the cat wouldn't face him. She would try to pounce on him when his back was turned, but she would never face a duel with that terrible bill.

'The result was that Mr Jackdaw – Lucifer we called him – got to be the boss of the roost round that stable-yard. He knew it, too. And everybody hated him.

'Well, one day Corky came to me just brimming over with news and excitement.

' "What *do* you think?" says he. "You know that new stable-lad, the cross-eyed one with red hair? – Well, he's making a trap to catch Lucifer. I saw him myself."

' "Oh," I said, "don't get excited over that. He'll never catch him. That bird knows every kind of trap that was ever invented."

"Nevertheless Corky was very hopeful. And he used to spend hours and days watching that red-headed lad trying to bag Mr Jackdaw. First the boy used a sieve and a string, baiting the arrangement with raw meat. But Lucifer gave that clumsy contrivance one glance and never even looked at it again. Next the lad rigged up various sorts of nets into which he hoped the bird would fly or could be driven. Corky kept running to me with reports, two or three times a day, to keep me posted on how things were going. Then horse-hair nooses were tried – and paper bags with raisins and treacle inside.

'But, as I had told Corky, Lucifer was a wily bird and he seemed to know just as much about traps as the boy did. What was more, he soon got on to the fact that Corky was watching the proceedings with great interest. Because one morning he chased him away from some soup-meat on the garbage heap, saying,

' "Hoping to see me get trapped, eh? You little imp! Get out of that before I nip the tail off you!"

' "You may get caught yet, you big black bully," Corky

threw back at him as he ran for a hole. "And I hope you do!"

'"Oh, hah, hah!" croaked the jackdaw as he set to on the meat. "That red-haired bumpkin couldn't catch me if he tried for a lifetime."

'But the red-haired bumpkin was a persevering lad and not so stupid as he looked. He had made up his mind that he was going to have that jackdaw in a cage for a pet. And after a good many failures, instead of giving up, he set to work observing the quarry and his habits and trying to find just why it was that he hadn't caught him. And among other things he noticed that the jackdaw had one favourite drinking-place, a little pool under a tap in a corner of the stable-yard. Also he noticed that the bird never flew down to settle where anything new had been set up or anything old taken away.

'In other words, the stable-lad had stumbled upon the truth that birds, like mice, are afraid of anything unfamiliar. That's their great protection. They've a keen sense of observation; and whenever a yard or a corner of a garden has anything new or changed about it, they are at once suspicious and on their guard.

'So, having learned this, the bumpkin went about his job differently. He saw that whatever was changed, whatever he put out to catch the jackdaw must be changed or put out gradually. He began by laying a twig down near the watering-place – just one. Lucifer, when he came, eyed it suspiciously. But finally he decided it was innocent, walked around it and took his drink. The next morning the boy had two twigs there. Lucifer behaved in the same way. Three mornings later there were four or five twigs there. And so on, until a regular little bank of twigs surrounded the tiny pool beneath the tap; and the jackdaw couldn't get at the water without stepping on them.

'But at this point Mr Lucifer became very wary. He walked all around the twigs several times and finally flew away. He had gone to find another drinking-place.

'Corky came to me in despair.

' "You are right," he said dolefully. "That bird is related to the Devil, I do believe. I'm afraid he'll never be caught."

'But suddenly the weather came to the assistance of our red-headed trapper. It was late November; and one morning we woke up to find the ground and everything covered with a white mantle of snow and every puddle, pool and stream topped with ice. Mr Jackdaw came into the stable-yard looking for breakfast – as usual. There wasn't any. Everything was covered, cold and silent. He looked in at the

stable door. There he saw us, nibbling oats on the top of the bin. He would have come in, only he was afraid.

' "You vermin," he sneered from the door, "are well off, guzzling in shelter, dry and warm, while honest folk can starve outdoors, with every blade of grass buried in the snow. A pest on the weather!"

' "We would throw you some oats," said I, "if you hadn't always been such a mean, selfish grouch to us, driving us from every titbit even when there was enough for all. Yes, you're right: it *is* bad weather – for folks who've gone through life making no friends." '

23

THE CUNNING OF LUCIFER,
THE JACKDAW

A T this point some of the old pensioners at the back of the hall made another request that the Stable Mouse should speak a little louder. John Dolittle suggested that she should be given a tea-canister or something to stand on, so that her voice would carry to the rear of the Assembly Room. After a short delay an empty mustard tin was found, which served the purpose very well. And as soon as she had climbed up on to it and overcome her embarrassment the speaker continued:

'The jackdaw made some vulgar remark in answer to what I had said and hopped away from the door. We got on to the window-sill and watched him flopping across the yard through the deep, loose, fluffy snow. I felt sort of sorry for him. I could see he was hungry; and in that weather he might not find a scrap to eat in a whole day. I was about to call him back and give him some oats, but Corky wouldn't let me.

'"Don't worry," said he. "He'll take care of himself. — Serve him right, the mean bully!"

'As he passed his old drinking-place the jackdaw just glanced at it, expecting to find it frozen like all the other water out of doors. But behold! It wasn't. As a matter of fact the red-haired lad had specially come and broken the ice even before Mr Jackdaw was abroad.

'Lucifer was just as thirsty as he was hungry. He floundered, half flying through the snow, towards the tap. Corky got dreadfully excited as he watched him. We both guessed that those twigs were some sort of trap – though

HUGH LOFTING

how they worked neither of us knew as yet. This morning
they were half covered with snow and looked like a regular
innocent part of the landscape. The water was very tempt-
ing. Lucifer hopped nearer. And Corky got even more
worked up.

'Finally Mr Jackdaw jumped up on to the mound of
twigs and took a long, long drink. Corky was disappointed.
Nothing seemed to happen. It looked as though whatever
machinery the twigs contained had failed to go off. And it
was only when the bird started to leave the drinking-place
that we realized what the trap was. The mound he was
standing on stuck to his feet. The twigs had been covered
with birdlime.

'Dear me, how he floundered and flopped and fluttered! And the more he fought and pulled and worked, the more the sticky twigs got gummed up with his feathers. We could see now that there were a whole lot of them beneath the snow; and by the time that the jackdaw had them all stuck to him it was quite clear that for the present he stood no chance whatever of flying or getting away.

'Then suddenly a door opened across the yard and the red-haired lad triumphantly came forth and took possession of the helpless Mr Lucifer. Whereupon Corky proceeded to do somersaults of joy all over the stable.

'Well, you can be sure there was general rejoicing throughout the stables and the farm-yard. For not only had Lucifer made himself objectionable to us, but he was thoroughly unpopular with every living thing in the whole neighbourhood.

'The lad put him in a wicker cage whose bars were reinforced with wire; and he hung the cage – of all places – in our stable: I am bound to say that once more I felt sorry for the bird. It was bad enough to be caught and imprisoned; but then to be put where other creatures, of whom he had made enemies, could look at him all day while they rejoiced in their freedom, did seem to me a bit too much.

'And, oh, what a state he was in, poor wretch! The bird-lime had made all his sleek plumage messy, so that he looked like some old silk hat brought in off the dust-heap. And for the first day he did nothing but bang his head against the bars trying to get out, so that he rubbed all the feathers off the top of his head and looked worse than ever.

'Corky, the heartless little imp, had a grand time sitting outside his cage and laughing at him. He had had to run away from Lucifer so often when he was free, he was deter-

mined to make up for it now that he had a chance. I thought this was mean and I told Corky so.

‘ "Besides," I said, "I'm still scared of him – even now."

‘ "Oh," said Corky, laughing, "what can he do, the big bully? He's caught now for good."

‘ "Just the same," I said, "be careful. He's clever, don't forget."

‘All day long the jackdaw never said a word, not even in answer to Corky's most spiteful remarks. There was something dignified, as well as pathetic, in his downfall. He had now given up beating himself against the bars and just sat there, all huddled up at the bottom of his cage, the picture of despair. The only thing about him that seemed alive at all was his gleaming eyes full of bitter hatred. They looked like coals of fire as they followed every movement of Corky and the other mice who were taunting him outside the cage.

'It is curious how heartless some creatures can be. After Lucifer had subsided like that, those little monkeys, Corky and his friends, got up on top of the cage and started dropping bits of mortar and putty down on the jackdaw's head. I tried my best to stop them, but there were too many of them and they wouldn't listen to me. Before long there must have been a good dozen gathered on top of the cage laughing and throwing things at their old enemy, the one-time bully of the stable-yard. Truly Lucifer was paying a terrible price for a selfish life.

'And, alas! my fears proved right. That terrible bird was still dangerous, even when he was shut up in a cage. While those little fools were playing their heartless game one afternoon I was cleaning up our home under the hay-loft floor. Suddenly I heard a dreadful shriek. I rushed out of the hole and bounded down through a trap door into the stable below.

'Corky's friends were all standing around the jackdaw's cage on the window-sill, their eyes popping out of their heads with horror. I looked for Corky among them. He wasn't there. On coming nearer I found that he was *inside* the cage firmly held in the jackdaw's right claw! As usual, he had been more daring than the rest. And as he had crawled over the cage he had come just a fraction of an inch too near the bird he was teasing. Like a flash – he told me this afterwards – Lucifer had thrust his long beak between the bars, caught him by the tail and pulled him inside. When I came up Corky was still bawling blue murder at the top of his voice.

' "Be quiet!" said the jackdaw. "Stop struggling or I'll

kill you right away. – Where's his wife?" he asked, turning to the others.

'"Here I am," said I, stepping up to the cage.

'"Good!" said he. "You are just in time to save your husband's life. I want a hole gnawed through the bottom of this cage right away – one big enough for me to get out of. Mice can eat through wood. I can't. There is room for you to get under – the legs of the cage are high enough. But please waste no time. That lad is likely to come back any moment."

'"But," I began, "it would take . . ."

'"Don't argue!" said he shortly. "If a hole isn't made in the bottom of this cage large enough for me to escape through before nightfall, I'll bite your husband's head off."

'Well, I could see he meant it. And the only thing for me to do was to obey – unless I wanted to be left a widow. Lucky for me it was that the other mice were standing round. I knew I could never nibble a hole alone, in so short a time, big enough for that great hulk to pass through. And, scared to death as Corky's brave friends were, I finally persuaded them to help me.

'With the jackdaw still firmly clutching his vitals, Corky watched us as we slipped under the floor of the cage and set to work.

'It wasn't easy. And if my husband's life hadn't depended on it I doubt very much whether it would have been done in time. The main difficulty was in getting started. As you all know – but perhaps the Doctor and Tommy do not – to begin biting a hole in the middle of a flat board is, even for a mouse, an almost impossible task. To chew off a corner, or to widen an old hole that has been already begun, that's different.

'However, I was desperate; and somehow – my teeth were sore for weeks afterwards – I got four holes started in the bottom of that cage, one in each corner, in the first quarter of an hour. Then I got eight other mice, two to each hole, to continue the work. As soon as one mouse's jaws got tired I took him off the job and put a fresh mouse on. I even went down into the foundations of the stables and gathered together all the mice I could find. Corky had always been popular with the neighbourhood; and as soon as they heard that his life was in danger they were willing enough to assist. In this way I had continuous relays of fresh help at work.

'Before very long we had those four holes very nearly joined up. There was only a little strip of wood scarcely

wider than a pencil keeping the bottom of that cage from falling right out, whole.

'The old jackdaw, still clutching his wretched victim, watched the work with an eagle eye. His plan was, as soon as the bottom fell, to turn the cage over on its side. This he could easily do directly he got his feet on the window-sill, because the cage wasn't very heavy.

'Well, we only just finished in time – in time for Corky, that is. Because I'm certain that if we had been interrupted before we had it done the jackdaw would have killed him. As the bottom of the cage clattered out Lucifer let go his victim at last, and with one twist of his powerful bill, not only threw the cage on its side, but hurled it right down to the stable floor – with Corky inside it.

'At that moment the lad came in and saw his precious pet standing, free, on the window-sill. He leapt to grab him. But Lucifer, with one curving swoop, skimmed neatly over his head and out through the stable door into the wide world; while all around the bewildered lad the mice, who had freed the bird whom they hated worse than poison, scuttled and scattered to safety.'

24

MOORSDEN MANOR

AT this point, before anyone was quite certain whether the Stable Mouse had finished her story or not, some sort of a commotion started at the back of the hall. There was a great deal of excited whispering and we could see that some new arrival had just turned up in a very breathless state. He seemed to be demanding to speak with the Doctor at once.

The white mouse, as president and chairman of the meeting, started for the back of the hall to see what all the excitement was about. But the newcomer was apparently in much too great a hurry to stand on ceremony, and before the white mouse had more than got out of his seat he could be seen elbowing his way through the crowd making for John Dolittle.

'Doctor,' he cried, 'there's a fire over at Moorsden Manor. It's in the cellar. And everybody's asleep and no one knows anything about it.'

'Good gracious!' cried the Doctor, rising and looking at his watch – 'Asleep! Is it as late as that? – Why, so it is.

Nearly an hour past midnight. What's in the cellar – wood, coal?'

'It's chock full of wood,' said the mouse. 'But the fire hasn't got to it yet – thank goodness! My nest, with five babies in it, is right in the middle of the wood pile. The wife thought the best thing I could do would be to come and tell you. Nobody else understands our language, anyway. She's staying with the children. The fire started in a heap of old sacks lying in a corner of the cellar. The place is full of smoke already. There is no chance of our carrying the babies out because there are too many cats about. Once the fire reaches the wood it's all up with us. Won't you come – quick, Doctor?'

'Of course I will,' said John Dolittle. He was already scrabbling his way out through the tunnel, nearly wrecking the Rat and Mouse Club on the way. 'Stubbins,' he called as he reached the top, 'go and wake Bumpo – and send Jip along to Matthew's house. We'd better get all the help we can. If the blaze hasn't gone too far we can probably get it under all right. Here's a note that Jip can give to Matthew, for the fire brigade – but it always takes them an eternity to get on the scene.'

He hastily scribbled a few words on an old envelope, with which I dashed off in one direction, while he disappeared in another.

For the next fifteen minutes I was occupied in getting Jip and then Bumpo aroused and informed of the situation. Bumpo was always the slowest man in the world to wake up. But after a good deal of hard work I managed to get him interested in clothes – and fires. Jip I had already sent trotting down the Oxenthorpe Road with his note to fetch Matthew to the scene.

Then I clutched Bumpo (still only half dressed and half awake) firmly by the hand and hurried off after the Doctor in the direction of the fire.

Now Moorsden Manor was the largest and most pretentious private residence in Puddleby. Like the Doctor's home, it was on the outskirts of the town and was surrounded by a large tract of its own land. Its present owner, Mr Sidney Throgmorton, was a middle-aged man who had only recently come into the property. His millionaire father had died the year before, leaving him this and several other handsome estates in different parts of England and Scotland. And many people had expressed surprise that he remained at the Manor all the year round when he had so many other castles and fine properties to go to.

The main gates to the estate were guarded by a lodge.

And when I arrived I found the Doctor hammering on the door trying to wake the lodge-keeper up. The gates, of course, were locked; and the whole of the grounds were enclosed by a high wall which was much too high to climb over.

Almost at the same moment that Bumpo and I got there Matthew Mugg, led by Jip, also arrived.

'Good gracious!' the Doctor was saying as he thumped the door with his fist. 'What sleepers! The whole place could burn down while we're standing here. Can it be that the lodge is empty?'

'No,' said Matthew. 'The keeper's here – or his wife. One of them is always on duty. That I know. I'll throw a stone against the window.'

It was only a small pebble that he threw, but the Cats'-meat-Man put such force behind it that it went right through the pane with a crash.

Indignant shouts from inside told us that at last we had succeeded in arousing some one. And a few moments later a man in a nightshirt, with a shotgun in one hand and a candle in the other, appeared at the door. As the Doctor stepped forward he quickly set the candle down and raised the gun as if to shoot.

'It's all right,' said John Dolittle. 'I've only come to warn you. There's a fire up at the Manor – in the cellar. The people must be roused at once. Let me through, please.'

'I will not let you through,' said the man stubbornly. 'I heard tell of hold-up gangs playing that game afore. The cheek of you, coming breaking into my windows this time of night! And how do you come to know what's going on up at the Manor?'

'A mouse told me about it,' said the Doctor. Then seeing the look of disbelief coming over the man's face, he added:

HUGH LOFTING

'Oh, don't argue with me! I *know* there's a fire there. Won't you please let us in?'

But the man had apparently no intention whatever of doing so. And I cannot say that he should be altogether blamed for that. For with Bumpo and Matthew we certainly must have seemed a queer delegation to call in the middle of the night.

Goodness only knows how long we would have stood there while the fire in the Manor cellar went on growing, if Matthew hadn't decided to deal with the situation in his own peculiar way. With a whispered word to Bumpo he suddenly ducked forward and wrenched the shotgun out of the lodge-keeper's hands. Bumpo grabbed the candle

that stood beside the door. And the fort was in our possession.

'Come on, Doctor,' said the Cats'-meat-Man. 'There's another door through here which leads into the grounds. We can't wait to talk things over with him. Maybe when the brigade comes along in an hour or so he will believe that there really is a fire.'

Bumpo had already found and opened the second door. And before the astonished keeper had had time to get his breath we were all through it and running up the drive that led to the big house.

'I suppose it will take us another age to get anyone awake here,' gasped the Doctor, as we arrived breathless

172

before the imposing portico and gazed up at the high double-doors.

'No, it won't,' said Matthew. And he let off the lodge-keeper's shotgun at the stars and started yelling 'Fire!' at the top of his voice. This din the Doctor, Bumpo and I added to by hammering on the panels and calling loudly for admittance.

But we did not have long to wait this time. The shotgun was a good alarm. Almost immediately lights appeared in various parts of the house. Next, several windows were thrown open and heads popped out demanding to know what was the matter.

'There's a fire,' the Doctor kept shouting – 'A fire in your house. Open the doors and let us in.'

A few minutes later the heavy bolts were shot back and an old man-servant with a candle opened the door.

'I can't find the master,' he said to the Doctor. 'He isn't in his room. He must have fallen asleep in some other part of the house. All the rest have been woken up. But I can't find the master.'

'Where's the cellar?' asked the Doctor, taking the candle and hurrying by him. 'Show me the way to the cellar.'

'But the master wouldn't be in the cellar, sir,' said the old man. 'What do you want in the cellar?'

'A family of mice,' said the Doctor – 'Young ones. They're in great danger. Their nest is in the wood-pile. Show me the way, quick!'

25

THE FIRE

I THINK that, for both the Doctor and myself, that was one of the most extraordinary nights we ever experienced. John Dolittle, as every one knows, had for a long time now taken no part whatever in the neighbourhood's human affairs. Ever since he had given up his practice as an ordinary doctor and come to be looked upon as a crank naturalist, he had accepted the reputation and retired from all social life. While he was pleasant and kind to every one, he avoided his neighbours even more than they avoided him.

And now suddenly, through this alarm of fire brought by the mouse from the Manor cellar, he found himself pitchforked by Fate, as it were, into a whole chain of happenings and concerns which he would have given a great deal to stay out of.

When Matthew, Bumpo and I followed him into the hall of the great house we found things in a pretty wild state of confusion. In various stages of dress and undress people were running up and down stairs, dragging trunks, throwing valuables over the banisters and generally behaving like a hen-roost in a panic. The smell of smoke was strong and pungent; and when more candles had been lit I could see that the hall was partly filled with it.

There was no need for the Doctor now to ask the way to the cellar. Over to the left of the hall there was a door leading downward by an old-fashioned winding stair. And through it the smoke was pouring upward at a terrible rate.

To my horror, the Doctor tied a handkerchief about his face, dashed through this doorway and disappeared into

the screen of smoke before anyone had time to stop him. Seeing that Bumpo and I had it in our minds to follow, Matthew held out his hand.

'Don't. You'd be more trouble than help to him,' he said. 'If you were overcome, the Doctor would have to fetch you up too. Let's get outside and break the cellar windows. It must be full of smoke down there – more smoke than fire, most likely. If we can let some of it out, maybe the Doctor can see what he's doing.'

With that all three of us ran for the front door. On the way we bumped into the old man-servant, who was still wandering aimlessly around, wringing his hands and wailing that he couldn't find 'the master'. Matthew grabbed him and shoved him along ahead of us into the front garden.

'Now,' said he, 'where are the cellar windows? – Quick, lead us to 'em!'

Well, finally we got the poor old doddering butler to take us to the back of the house where, on either side of the kitchen door, there were two areas with cellar windows in them. To his great astonishment and horror we promptly proceeded to kick the glass out of them. Heavy choking smoke immediately belched forth into our faces.

'Hulloa there! – Doctor!' gasped Matthew. 'Are you all right?'

The Cats'-meat-Man had brought a bull's-eye lantern with him. He shone it down into the reeking blackness of the cellar. For a few moments, which seemed eternally long, I was in an agony of suspense waiting for the answering shout that didn't come. Matthew glanced upward over his shoulder.

'Humph!' he grunted with a frown. 'Looks as though we'll have to organize a rescue party by the stair.'

But just as he was about to step up out of the area I clutched him by the arm.

'Look!' I said, pointing downward.

And there in the beam of his lantern a hand could be seen coming through the reeking hole in the broken window. It was the Doctor's hand. And in the hollow of the half-open palm five pink and hairless baby mice were nestling.

'Well, for the love of Methuselah!' muttered Matthew, taking the family and passing them up to me.

The Doctor's hand withdrew and almost immediately reappeared again, this time with the thoroughly frightened mother-mouse – whom I also pocketed.

But Matthew didn't wait for the Doctor's hand to go back for anything else. He grabbed it by the wrist and with

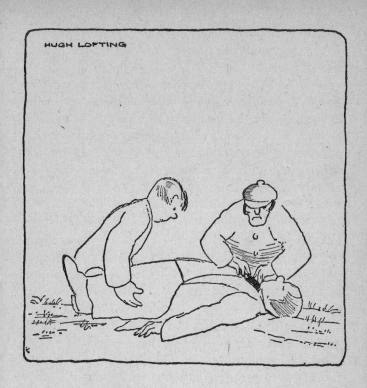

a mighty heave pulled John Dolittle, with the window-sash and all, up into the area. We saw at once that he was staggering and in pretty bad condition: and we half dragged, half lifted him out away from the choking smoke, to a lawn near by. Here we stretched him out flat and undid his collar.

But before we had time to do anything else for him he began to struggle to his feet.

'I'm all right,' he gasped. 'It was only the smoke. We must get a bucket chain started. The fire has just reached the wood pile. It it's allowed to get a good hold the whole place will burn down.'

There is not the least doubt that that mouse who brought

the news of the fire to the Doctor saved Moorsden Manor from total destruction – and possibly several lives as well. Certainly if it had not been for our efforts the place would never have been saved by those living there, even if they had been awakened in time. I never saw such an hysterical crew in my life. Everybody gave advice and nobody did anything. And the head of the servants, the old white-haired butler, continued to dodder around getting in every one's way, still asking if the master had been seen yet.

However, without waiting for assistance from anyone else, the Doctor, Matthew, Bumpo and I formed a bucket line on our own, and by it we conveyed from the kitchen sink a continuous supply of water to those burning sacks and firewood. And before very long nothing remained but a charred and hissing mass of what had promised to be a very serious conflagration.

In addition to this Matthew discovered a tap in the garden, and with the help of a hose which we got out of the stable we brought another stream into the cellar through the broken window, which could be kept in constant readiness if the fire should break out again.

While we were attaching the hose in the garden a man suddenly appeared out of a shrubbery and accosted the Doctor in a distinctly unfriendly manner.

'Who are you?'

'I?' said the Doctor, a little taken aback. 'I'm John Dolittle. Er – and you?'

'My name is Sidney Throgmorton,' said the man. 'And I would like to know what you mean by breaking into my lodge at this hour of night, smashing windows and assaulting the keeper.'

'Why, good gracious!' said the Doctor. 'We wanted to warn you about the fire. We hadn't time to stand on ceremony. The keeper wouldn't let us in. As it was, we only

just got here in time. I think I can assure you that if we *hadn't* got here the house would have been burned to the ground.'

I now saw in the gloom behind the man's shoulder that the lodge-keeper was with him.

'You have acted in a very high-handed manner, sir,' said Sidney Throgmorton. 'My lodge-keeper has his orders as to whom he shall, and whom he shall not, admit. And there is a fire department in the town whose business it is to look after conflagrations. For you to thrust your way into my home in this violent and unwarrantable manner, in the middle of the night, is nothing short of a scandal, sir – for which I have a good mind to have you arrested. I will ask you and your friends to leave my premises at once.'

26

THE LEATHER BOXES

FOR a moment or two the Doctor was clearly about to reply. I could see by the dim light of Matthew's lantern the anger and mortification struggling in his face. But finally he seemed to feel that to a man of this nature no words of explanation or justice would mean anything.

And certainly this Throgmorton person was an extraordinary individual. From his speech he seemed fairly well educated. But the whole of his bloated, red-faced appearance was as vulgar and as unprepossessing as it could be.

'My coat is in your cellar,' said the Doctor quietly at last. 'I will get it. Then we will go.'

To add insult to injury, the man actually followed us down into the cellar, as though we might steal something if we were not watched. Here lamps were still burning which we had lit to help us in making sure that there were no sparks of fire left that might smoulder up again. The man muttered some expression of annoyance beneath his breath when he saw the water which flooded the floor.

At this last show of ingratitude for what we had done, Bumpo could contain his indignation no longer.

'Why, you discourteous and worm-like boor!' he began, advancing upon Throgmorton with battle in his eye.

'*Please!* Bumpo!' the Doctor interrupted. 'No further words are necessary. We will go.'

By the brighter light of the lamps I now saw that Throgmorton carried beneath his arm several small leather boxes. In climbing up over the wood pile, in order to see what damage we might have done on the other side, he laid these down for a moment on top of a wine cask. I was close to

Matthew. In the fraction of a second, while Throgmorton's back was turned, I saw the Cat's-meat-Man open the upper one of the boxes, glance into it and shut it again.

The box contained four enormous diamond shirt-studs.

As soon as he had his coat the Doctor wasted no further time, but made his way, with us following him, up the stairs and out of the house which he had saved from destruction.

The keeper accompanied us to the lodge and let us out. Matthew, like Bumpo, was just burning to speak his mind even to this representative of the establishment which had shown us such discourtesy. But the Doctor seemed determined that there should be no further controversy and checked him every time he tried to open his mouth.

However, at the gate we met the fire brigade coming to the rescue. This was too much for Matthew's self-control, and he called to them as we stepped out on to the road:

'Oh, turn around and go back to bed! We put that fire out before you'd got your boots on.'

Outside the boundaries of the Moorsden Manor estate not even the Doctor could stay the tide of Matthew's and Bumpo's indignant eloquence.

'Well, of all the good-for-nothing, mangy, lowdown ingrates,' the Cat's-meat-Man began, 'that stuffed pillow of a millionaire takes the prize! After all we've done for him! Getting up out of our beds, working like hosses – all to keep his bloomin' mansion from burning down. And then he tells us we've ruined his cellar by pouring water into it!'

'Such a creature,' said Bumpo, 'would make anyone feel positively rebellious. In Oxford he would not be allowed, under any circumstances, to proceed farther with his obnoxious existence. It was only with the greatest difficulty that I restrained myself from hitting him on the bono publico.'

'Enough,' said the Doctor. 'Please don't say any more. I am trying to forget it. The whole affair is just one of those incidents which it is no use thinking about or getting yourself worked up over afterwards. I'm often very grateful that life has made it possible for me to keep away from my neighbours and mind my own business. This occasion couldn't be helped – but it has made me more grateful still. Thank goodness, anyway, that we got the mice out all right before the fire reached them. You have them safely in your pocket, Stubbins, have you not?'

'Yes,' said I, putting my hand in to make sure. 'Oh, but, Doctor, your hat? Where is it? You've left it behind.'

John Dolittle raised his hand to his bare head.

'Dear me!' said he. 'What a nuisance! – Well, I'll have to go back, that's all.'

I knew how he hated to. But the well-beloved headgear was too precious. In silence all four of us turned about.

The gate was still open from the arrival of the fire brigade. Unchallenged, we walked in and down the drive towards the house.

Half-way along the avenue the Doctor paused.

'Perhaps it would be as well,' said he, 'if you waited for me here. After all, there is no need for four of us to come to fetch a hat.'

He went on alone while we stood in the shadow of the

trees. The moon had now risen and we could see more plainly.

I noticed that Matthew was restless and fidgety. He kept muttering to himself and peering after the Doctor down the drive. Presently in a determined whisper he jerked out:

'No. I'm blessed if I let him go alone! I don't trust that Mr Throgmorton. Come on, you chaps. Let's follow the Doctor. Keep low, behind the trees. Don't let yourselves be seen. But I've a notion he may need us.'

I had no idea what was in Matthew's mind. But from experience I knew that usually when he acted on impulse, without rhyme or reason like this, he acted rightly. I always put it down to some mysterious quality he inherited with his gipsy blood.

So like a band of Indian scouts, scuttling from tree to tree, we shadowed the Doctor up the avenue drive till he came to the clearing before the house. Here the fire brigade, with a great deal of pother and fuss, was in the act of departing – after its captain had made sure that the fire was really out. The big door lamps, either side of the portico, had been lighted and the courtyard was fairly well illumined. Mr Throgmorton could be seen dismissing the firemen and their worthy captain. We saw John Dolittle go up to him, but he pretended to be too busy to attend to anything but the business of the fire brigade.

And it was only after the engine and fire-escape had clattered noisily away, leaving the courtyard empty save for him and the Doctor, that he deigned to notice John Dolittle's presence. This time he did not wait for the Doctor to speak.

'You here again!' he shouted. 'Didn't I tell you to get off the premises? Clear out of here, or I'll set the dogs on you.'

'I've come back for my hat,' said the Doctor, controlling

HUGH LOFTING

himself with truly wonderful restraint. 'It's in the hall.'

'Get out of here!' the other repeated threateningly. 'I'll have no more of you suspicious characters messing round my place tonight. I find you smashed the windows in the cellar as well as the lodge. Clear out, unless you want the dogs after you.'

'I will not go,' said the Doctor firmly, 'until I have my hat.'

('My goodness! But I'd love to give that fellow a crack on the jaw!' whispered Matthew, who was standing behind the same tree as myself.)

The Doctor's answer seemed to infuriate Throgmorton beyond all bounds. He drew a whistle from his pocket and blew upon it loudly. An answering shout came from some-where in the darkness of the gardens.

'Let go Dina and Wolf!' called Throgmorton.

('That's his two man-killing mastiffs,' chuckled Matthew in my ear. 'I know 'em – regular savages. He keeps 'em to defend the place. Now we'll see some fun.')

27

THE WATCH-DOGS

NEXT moment we heard a scraping rush of paws upon the gravel and two gigantic dogs bounded out of the gloom into the lighted courtyard.

'Grab 'im! – Go get 'im!' shouted Throgmorton. To-gether the two dogs hurled themselves towards the figure of the stranger. Then Mr. Throgmorton got a great sur-prise. The stranger did not run or indeed show any panic whatever. But as he turned his face in the direction of the on-coming dogs he made some curious sounds, almost like another kind of growl answering theirs.

At this the two hounds behaved in a most curious manner. Instead of grasping their prey by the throat, they wagged their tails, licked his hand and generally carried on as though he were no stranger at all, but a very old and dear friend of theirs. Then, in response to an order he gave them, they disappeared into the darkness from which they had come.

Beside me, behind the tree, Matthew covered his face with his hand to keep from laughing.

'I will now get my hat,' said the Doctor. And he walked calmly into the house.

As for Throgmorton, he was just speechless with rage.

It had been his proud boast that these two mastiffs, Dina and Wolf, had, between them, killed a burglar who had once attempted to rob the Manor. To be made ridiculous like this by such a quiet small person was more than he could bear.

Within the hall the Doctor could now be seen on his way out – with the precious hat. Throgmorton withdrew into the shadow of a door-column and waited.

'Yes, I thought so!' muttered Matthew. And he slid like a shadow out from behind the tree and crept towards the figure of the waiting Throgmorton.

John Dolittle, unaware of anything beyond the fact that he was anxious to get away from this disagreeable establishment as soon as possible, stepped briskly forth on to the gravel. An enormous weight landed on his shoulders and bore him to the ground.

'I'll teach you,' growled Throgmorton, 'to walk in and out of my house as though you – '

But he got no further, for Matthew had landed on top of him just as he had landed on the Doctor.

But Sidney Throgmorton, in spite of his bloated, unwholesome appearance, was a heavy, powerful man. He rose and threw Matthew off as though he were a fly. And he was just about to aim a kick at the Doctor lying on the ground when he suddenly found himself gripped from behind and lifted off his feet like a doll.

Indeed Bumpo, softly crooning his favourite African battle-song, not only lifted him, but was now proceeding to carry his portly victim bodily away towards the building.

'Well!' said the Doctor, rising and brushing his clothes, 'what an offensive person! Who would ever have thought he'd do that! The man must be out of his senses. – Oh, Bumpo! Stop, stop, for Heaven's sake!'

John Dolittle leapt forward – and only just in time. For the Crown Prince of the Jollinginki was apparently just on the point of knocking Mr Throgmorton's brains out on his own doorstep.

'Well, but,' said he as the Doctor grabbed him,' 'is he not a useless and unsightly cucumbrance to the earth? – Permit me, Doctor. A little tap on the geranium and all will be well.'

'No, no,' said the Doctor quickly. 'You're not in Africa now, Bumpo. Put him down and let us be going.'

'I'll have you all in jail for this,' grunted Throgmorton, as Bumpo let him fall heavily, like a large sack of potatoes, to the ground.

'If you take my tip,' grinned Matthew, 'you'll keep your silly mouth shut. There's three witnesses here saw you make that attack on the Doctor – slinkin' up and waitin' for him behind the doorpost. And don't forget, his honesty is as well known as yours, you know – maybe better – even if folks do call him a crank. Your money can't do everything.'

'And I have witnesses, too,' spluttered the other, 'who saw you all breaking into my lodge and using violence on the keeper.'

'Yes, to save your hide and your house from burning,' added Matthew. 'Go on and do your worst. I dare you to take it to any court.'

'Come, come!' said the Doctor, herding us away like children. 'Let us be going. No more, Matthew – please! Come, Bumpo!'

And leaving the fuming, spluttering master of the Manor to pick himself up from the gravel, we walked down the drive.

On the return walk all four of us were silent – also a little tired, for, as Matthew had said, we had worked hard at our thankless task. And we must have been more than half-way to the house before anyone spoke. It was the Cats'-meat-Man.

'You know,' said he, breaking out suddenly, 'there's something fishy about the whole thing. That's my opinion.'

'How do you mean?' said the Doctor sleepily, trying to show polite interest.

'About his ingratitude,' said Matthew, 'his wanting to get us off the place in such a hurry and – and, well, his general manner. I don't believe he ever thought we were suspicious characters at all – maybe the lodge-keeper might have, but not the owner. Why, everyone in Puddleby knows you, Doctor – even if you don't mix in with the society tea-parties and the afternoon muffin-worries.... And then the way things was run, up at the house there: nobody in charge unless the "master" is on the job. And the master wasn't. ... Why wasn't he? What was he doing all that time while old Moses was runnin' round hollerin' for him? ... And why –'

'Oh, Matthew,' the Doctor broke in, 'what's the use of guessing and speculating about it? Personally, I must confess I don't care what he was doing – or what he ever will do. Thank goodness, the whole stupid affair is over!'

But Matthew was much too wrapped up in his subject to dismiss it like that. And though he kept his voice low, as if he were talking to himself, he continued a quite audible one-man conversation for the rest of the way home.

'Yes, there's a mystery there, all right. And if anybody was to get to the bottom of it I'll bet they'd get a shock. ... Why, even the lodge-keeper – there's another queer thing: supposing he *was* scared by the way we woke him up, just the same, no man in his senses – orders or no orders – is going to take no notice of a fire alarm. If he didn't want to let us in, he could anyway call to his wife and send her up to the Manor to find out. And then when he does follows us up to the house, and sees that there really is a fire, does he do anything to help us put it out? No, he does not. He goes and tells the precious "master" how badly we treated him getting in to save 'em all from burning to death. And, by the way, that's still another queer thing: how did he know where to find the master? The old butler didn't know – no, nor nobody else.'

The Doctor sighed gratefully as we finally reached the little gate. After this hard and trying night the thought of a good bed was very pleasant – as was also the prospect of getting a respite from Matthew's thinking aloud.

28

THE SCRAP OF PARCHMENT

THE rescued mouse family which I had brought home in my pocket were given quarters in the club. The white mouse personally saw to it that the very best furnished suite was given to them. And, of course, they immediately became public heroes in Mouse Town. The thrilling story they had to tell of the fire; the father-mouse's midnight gallop for help; their perilous rescue by John Dolittle himself; and finally the Doctor's treatment at the hands of the churlish owner of the Manor, was undoubtedly the sensation of the season.

Many of the members were so infuriated over the discourtesy shown to the Doctor that they wanted to organize a campaign of revenge – which would, I believe, have utterly ruined the Manor if they had been allowed to carry it out. For they planned to chew up the curtains, drill the panelling, eat holes in the tapestries, break the wine glasses, and a whole lot of other mischief which rats and mice can easily accomplish if they want to. But to their indignation, as to Matthew's, the Doctor turned a deaf ear. He wanted to forget it.

Nevertheless, in the Rat and Mouse Club Throgmorton's

ingratitude and his scandalous behaviour continued for a long time the principal topic of conversation. And any mice from the Manor who dropped in of an evening were always the centre of attention while they stayed, so great was the public interest in gossip from that quarter.

And it was through this that the poor Doctor, despite his earnest desire to stay out of the affairs of Sidney Throgmorton or any other neighbours, found himself finally forced by circumstances to take further part in matters which he insisted were 'none of his business'.

It began by the white mouse coming to me one night and saying:

'There's a mouse just run over from the Manor who

has lived up there for some time. He has something he wants to show the Doctor. But the poor man is always so busy I thought I'd speak to you first. Will you come down to the club and see him?'

'All right,' I said. And I left what I was doing and went down right away.

When I got into the Assembly Room I found a whole crowd of members gathered around a mouse who seemed quite pleased with the sensation he was creating. They were all staring at a torn scrap of paper about the size of a visiting-card.

'I thought this might be of importance,' said the mouse to me. 'Of course I can't read what it says on it. But it is made of a very unusual kind of paper. That's a subject I do know something about, paper. I wondered whether the Doctor ought to see it. Perhaps you can tell us.'

I examined the slip. It was nibbled irregularly all round the edges like any piece of paper would be that had been part of a mouse's nest. But it was true: the paper itself was of a special kind. It was real parchment. Then I read the few words which were written in four lines across the scrap of parchment.

Well, after that I decided that the Doctor ought to see it. And without further ado I took it to him and told him so.

Matthew happened to be with him in the study at the time. And in spite of the fact that he couldn't read, he became quite interested as soon as he heard where the paper had come from.

'But what made the mouse think it would be of importance?' asked the Doctor, as he took it from me and put on his spectacles.

'On account of the nature of the paper,' I said. 'It's real parchment, the kind they use for special legal documents.'

While the Doctor was reading the few words written on the torn scrap I watched his face carefully. And I felt sure from his expression that he guessed what I had guessed. But he evidently wasn't going to admit it. Rather hurriedly he handed it back to me.

'Yes, er – quite interesting, Stubbins,' said he, turning to his work at the table. 'I'm rather busy just now. You'll excuse me, won't you?'

This was his polite way of telling me to go away and not bother him. And in the circumstances I felt there wasn't anything else for me to do but go.

Matthew's interest, on the other hand, was growing rather than diminishing. And as I left the room he followed me out. 'What do you make of that, Tommy?' he asked as soon as we had closed the door behind us.

'Why, between ourselves, Matthew,' said I, 'I think it's a will – or rather a piece of one. What's more, I believe the Doctor thinks so, too. But it is quite clear that he doesn't want to have anything to do with it. And nobody can blame him, after all he had to put up with from that horrible Throgmorton.'

'A will?' said Matthew. 'Whose will?'

'We don't know,' I said. 'This is all we have, just a corner of it.'

'A will, eh?' he muttered again. 'I wonder where that would fit in. . . . Humph!'

'What do you mean, fit in?' I asked.

'Into the puzzle,' he said, staring at the floor rapt in thought.

'I don't understand you, Matthew,' said I, rather impatiently. 'What puzzle?'

'I'll tell you later,' said he, 'after I've found out a little more. But I knew I was right. There *was* a mystery in that house. Keep that piece of paper carefully.'

And at that he left me, with the scrap of parchment in my hand, pondering over his words.

29

THE COMING OF KLING

FOR several days after that I saw nothing of Matthew. Moreover, while I was deeply interested in what he had said, I had very little time to think further of his 'mystery'. For I was kept exceptionally busy with my ordinary duties

HUGH LOFTING

as Assistant Manager of the Dolittle Zoo, in general – and in particular with the arrival of Kling.

Kling, who later came to be known among us as 'The Detective Dog', was such an unusual animal that I feel I ought to devote a little space to telling how he came to join the zoo.

One day while Jip was wandering around the streets on his own, as he often did, he came upon a mongrel terrier who was evidently very ill. He was lying in a corner by a wall, groaning pitifully.

'What's the matter?' said Jip, going up to him.

'I've just eaten a rat,' said the dog. 'And I have a dreadful stomach-ache.'

'My gracious!' said Jip. 'Eating rats at this season! Don't you know any better than that? You should never eat rats when there isn't an *R* in the month. Why, they're rank poison!'

'What's the *R* mean?' asked the mongrel, groaning again.

'Why, *Rats* of course,' said Jip. 'Come along to the Doctor at once. He'll soon give you something that will put your stomach right. What's your name?'

'Kling,' said the mongrel. 'Thanks, but I'm afraid I'm too ill to walk.'

'All right, Kling,' said Jip. 'You wait here and I'll go and get the Doctor.'

Jip dashed away at top speed, muttering to himself that he must speak to John Dolittle about instituting a Dog Ambulance for urgent cases of this kind.

When he got to the house he found that the Doctor was out. So he came to me instead. Together we hurried off at once to the rescue of the sick mongrel.

I saw right away that the patient was pretty far gone and that it would need very prompt treatment to save him. I gathered him up in my arms, sent Jip off to scour the town for the Doctor and hurried back as fast as I could to the house.

There I found that John Dolittle had returned during my absence. I rushed the patient into the surgery, where the Doctor immediately examined him.

'It's a case of poisoning,' he said. 'Very likely the rat you ate had been poisoned. But we can put you right again. You had better stay here for a few days. You can sleep in the parlour – where I'll be able to keep an eye on you. Here, drink this. Now, Stubbins, carry him in to the sofa and put some blankets over him. He has a temperature and mustn't get chilled. Tell me, Kling, how did you come to eat a rat?'

'I was starving,' said the mongrel rather shamefacedly. 'Hadn't had a meal for two days.'

'Well, next time,' said the Doctor, 'come round to our zoo – The Home for Cross-bred Dogs, you know. You can always get a meal there. But please, *don't* eat rats.'

Quite early the following morning I heard a most extraordinary noise in the Doctor's bedroom. It sounded as though he were moving every piece of furniture from its usual position and generally turning the place upside down. I was about to go up to see what was the matter, when he opened his door and called to me.

'Oh, Stubbins, have you seen anything of a boot of mine? I can't find it anywhere – the left one.'

'No, Doctor,' I said, 'I haven't.'

'It's most peculiar,' said he. 'I could have sworn I left it – both of them – beside the bed last night, just where I always take them off.'

My own first duty that morning was, of course, to see how the new patient, Kling, was getting on. And as soon as I got downstairs I went straight to the parlour. Imagine my astonishment to find the sofa empty and the patient gone!

Utterly puzzled, I wandered out through the French window into the garden. And there, in the middle of the lawn, I found not only Kling, but the Doctor's boot as well – which the new patient was thoughtfully chewing. As I ran to him, the Doctor also arrived, with his remaining boot on one foot and a bright red slipper on the other.

'Good gracious!' said John Dolittle. 'You made a quick recovery, Kling. I didn't give you permission to get up yet. What are you doing with my boot?'

There was really no need to ask. Even before the Doctor stooped and picked it up anyone could see that the dog had chewed a large hole in the side.

'Dear me!' said John Dolittle. 'Just look at that! Now what shall I do?'

'Oh, did you want those boots?' said Kling apologetically. 'I'm dreadfully sorry, Doctor. I thought they were an old pair you had thrown away.'

'Oh, no,' said the Doctor. 'They're my best boots – my only boots, in fact. Listen, Stubbins: after breakfast, would you mind running down with this to your father? Give him my compliments and ask him if he would be good enough to patch it while you wait. I've got to go up to town tonight to address a meeting of the Zoological Society, and I can't very well go in red slippers. ... But tell me, Kling: how comes it that you still chew boots? You're no longer a puppy, you know.'

'No,' said Kling, 'that's true. But I've never got out of the habit since my childhood days. It is strange, I know. My mother always said it meant I was a genius; but my father said it was clearly a sign I was just a plain fool and would never grow up.'

'Well, Kling,' said the Doctor, 'I suppose I'll have to get you a pair of shoes of your own to chew. I can't let you have mine, you know. Er – would you prefer brown or black?'

'Brown, please,' said Kling. 'They usually taste better. And would you mind if I had them buttoned instead of laced. I find chewing the buttons off almost the best part – very soothing.'

'Certainly,' said the Doctor. 'But we may find it hard to get brown buttoned boots in Puddleby. It's not a very up-to-date shopping centre, you understand. Perhaps you had better come with me. It's no use my buying you a pair of shoes that doesn't suit you. And I doubt if they will change them after you've tried them on – on your teeth, I mean.'

So that was how John Dolittle added yet another story to his reputation in the neighbourhood for eccentricity and craziness. After breakfast, while I took his damaged boot to my father's to be repaired, he took the mongrel Kling to the largest shoe shop in the town to buy him a pair of boots. The salesman was somewhat slow in getting it into his head that the customer (who was wearing slippers) wanted the shoes for the dog and not for himself. And for a whole week afterwards he entertained the neighbouring shopkeepers by telling them how the Doctor had requested that all the brown buttoned boots in the shop be set out in a row on the floor; and how this ill-conditioned, half-bred dog had then, at the Doctor's invitation, gone down the line and made his selection.

Kling himself insisted that his rapid recovery from the severe attack of ptomaine poisoning was largely aided by the soothing effect of chewing brown shoe leather. And certainly by that evening he seemed entirely himself and was frisking round the garden as lively as a puppy.

'Chewing a new pair of boots always makes me feel young again,' said he, leaping over the flower beds.

The whole of the Doctor's household as well as all the members of the Home for Cross-bred Dogs and the Dolittle Zoo took to Kling at once. And both the Doctor and I agreed that we had never met a more interesting personality in dogs – in spite of his juvenile fondness for boots. He was a good example of that rule which John Dolittle had more than once maintained: that the mongrels often have more character than the thoroughbreds. And it was, I think, greatly to the credit of our whole establishment that none of the other animals (not even Toby, the privileged) showed the least jealousy over the great popularity that Kling enjoyed from the first day of his joining the zoo.

30

THE MYSTERY OF MOORSDEN
MANOR

O F course it was not long after I had taken the scrap of torn parchment to John Dolittle that the white mouse came to me demanding to know what the Doctor had said about it. I had to disappoint him terribly by telling him that he had refused to show any interest in it whatever.

Jip was in my room at the time that the white mouse called. He had never quite forgiven me for having him sent back home the night of the fire – especially after he had learned later that there had been a fight and that his beloved Doctor had been treated discourteously by Throgmorton.

It was after supper, about half-past eight. And while the white mouse and I were talking the Cats'-meat-Man also dropped in. I had not seen him for several days.

'Well, Matthew,' I said, 'how are you getting on with your mystery?'

'Humph!' he muttered, sinking into an arm-chair. 'It's still a mystery all right.'

Jip cocked up his ears at that and wanted to know what we were talking about. I explained to him, in dog language, that Matthew Mugg was sure from certain things he had observed that night at the Manor that there was some mystery connected with the house and its owner.

'Tommy,' said Matthew, 'I can't get much forrarder until we find the rest of that will.'

'I'm afraid that may be hard,' said I, 'from the inquiries I've made.'

'Listen,' the white mouse whispered to me: 'I can get that mouse from the Manor for you any time you want.'

'All right,' I said. 'Send for him, will you, please? There's always a chance that he may have found out something since.'

Thereupon the white mouse disappeared, and Matthew and I went on with our conversation.

But it could not have been more than a quarter of an hour before the white mouse was back at my elbow again. And with him he had the mouse who had brought us the scrap of parchment.

'Tell me,' I said to the Manor mouse, 'did you ever find out anything more about the rest of that paper?'

'As it happens,' said he, 'I did – tonight. The scrap, as I told you, had been in a mouse nest – an old one which I had discovered by accident and taken to pieces. You see, I was going to rebuild it into a new one for myself. Well, this evening I met the owner of that old nest.'

'Ah!' I said. 'That sounds like news. And what did he tell you?'

'Well,' said the Manor mouse, 'the reason I hadn't met him before – as you know, I had made inquiries of all the rats and mice in the mansion – was that he had moved out of the house to a sort of potting-shed place in the garden. I happened to go out there looking for last year's chestnuts; and that's how I ran into him. He's very, very old – quite feeble in fact. But he had lived longer in the Manor than any of us.'

'Yes,' I said, 'but get on to the business of the parchment. What did he tell you about that?'

'It seems that it was in the days of this Mr Throgmorton's father when, he told me, he had lived in the old man's study on the first floor. He was building a nest for himself and his wife, and he made it behind the panelling – between the panelling and the wall. Nesting materials were hard to find. And he got into old Mr Throgmorton's desk – by drilling a hole through the back – and went through all the drawers looking for stuff he could use to make a nest of. Papers and red tape were about all he could find. And among the papers he chewed corners off, there was this large sheet which the old man kept locked up in the top drawer. My friend used it for a foundation for his nest because he saw it was nice and thick and would keep the draughts out. It seems the old man considered the paper important, because when, a few days later, he opened the drawer and found the corner chewed off, he swore and carried on something dreadful. This mouse was watching from behind the clock on the mantelpiece, and he says he never saw anyone get so angry. The old man saw right away that it was the work of mice, from the way in which the paper was nibbled. He hunted high and low for that missing corner – turned all the furniture in the whole room inside out. But of course he didn't find it because it was behind the panelling in my friend's nest. At last he gave it up and took the larger piece of the parchment away and hid it somewhere else.'

'Where ?' I asked, rising half out of my chair.

'The old mouse said he didn't know. But wherever it was, it wasn't in the study.'

I sank back disappointed.

'Do you think,' I asked, 'that if all the mice in the house went to work on it they could find it for us ?'

The Manor mouse shook his head.

'As a matter of fact,' said he, 'we have tried. As soon as we learned from the gossip at the Club that you were interested in the paper we began a search on our own. But no trace of it could we find.'

I translated for Matthew's benefit what the Manor

mouse had said, and his disappointment was even greater than mine.

'But tell me, Matthew,' I said, 'didn't you succeed in finding anything out yourself? When last I saw you you were going to do some investigating on your own account.'

'It wasn't so easy,' said he, 'for this reason: when the old man died and this Mr Throgmorton came into the property, all the servants were changed. That's suspicious in itself, of course. So trying to find out much about the family from gossip and hearsay was kind of hard. I learned some things, but nothing that seemed to help solve the problem.'

At this point Jip came up to my chair and nudged my knee beneath the table.

'Tommy,' said he, 'for solving problems the best hands I know are Cheapside and Kling.'

'Humph!' I muttered. 'Cheapside I could understand, because he is in touch with the gossip of the street sparrows. But why Kling? Why should he be good at solving problems?'

'Why, my gracious!' said Jip. 'He knows an awful lot about crime and the – er – underworld and all that. He belonged to a thief once.'

'To a thief!' I cried.

'Yes. You ought to get him some time to tell you the story of his life. You never heard anything so thrilling. When he was quite a puppy he was stolen by a sort of tramp person who specially trained him in all sorts of queer dodges. This tramp used to walk through the streets with Kling on a string. And to anybody passing who looked well-off, he'd say, "Do you want to buy a dog?" And they would usually say "Yes" in the end, because Kling had been taught all manner of cunning tricks with which to fascinate them. Then Kling, after he'd been sold, would run away from the new owner and come back to the tramp. He was trained to do that too, you see. And then the tramp would take him away to a new town and sell him over again. Kling says that man once sold him twelve times in one month. But later the tramp invented another way to make money even faster. He trained Kling to learn the geography of the new houses he went to, and especially where the silver and valuables were kept. And the tramp would come later and rob the house, Kling acting as guide for him and showing him over the place. Then together they would go off again to a new town.'

'Goodness me!' I said. 'What an awful record!'

'Yes,' said Jip. 'But Kling had no idea he was doing wrong, until one day he got talking about his adventures to a parson's dog, who was highly scandalized and persuaded him to give up the life of crime. So Kling, in spite of the fact that the tramp had always treated him kindly, ran away the first chance he got and never went back to him again.

'Oh my, yes, Kling's awfully well up on crime! You see, in his life with the tramp he fell in with many queer birds, regular gangs of crooks, you know. And in that way he learned a lot about the tricks and dodges of different kinds of criminals. And then later he got a job as a police dog in Belgium and he was used to hunt down lawbreakers. Why, in Brussels, I understand, he was known as "The Dog Detective". Had no end of a reputation. But he didn't care for that work, and after a year or so he ran away again. Then for a while he was a tramp himself – a dog tramp – said he wanted to see the world. He's had a wonderful career. And you'd never think it – unassuming and quiet, the way he is. On first meeting him one might almost think he was stupid, dragging that chewed-up shoe of his round. But I feel sure that if you and Matthew have a problem you want to solve you couldn't do better than consult Kling.'

'Yes, I believe you're right, Jip,' I said. 'Go and ask him if he'll come and talk to us, will you? Don't say anything about it to the other members of the Home for Cross-bred Dogs. You know how enthusiastic they get. But if you happen to see Cheapside in the garden ask him to drop in too, will you?'

While Jip was gone I explained to Matthew roughly what it was we proposed to do. Kling hadn't met Matthew yet, having arrived during the few days while the Cats'-meat-Man had been off 'investigating', as he called it.

But when, followed by Jip, the Detective Dog strolled into the room carrying one of his new chewing-boots, I thought I saw Matthew start almost uneasily. Kling too behaved in a rather odd manner. He stared hard at Matthew a moment through half-closed lids, as though he were try-ing to remember something. Then with a shake of his shoulders he settled down on the floor and began turning his boot over between his paws to find a good place to chew. Jip shot a glance at me that spoke volumes.

Knowing that Matthew didn't understand dog talk, I began by asking Kling if he had ever seen him before.

The mongrel thoughtfully pulled a button off his boot before answering.

'Oh, well,' he said, 'what does it matter! He's a friend of yours – and the Doctor's. I've met an awful lot of people, you know. After all, a man's past is his own. I believe in letting bygones be bygones. . . . Jip tells me you have some-thing you wanted to see me about.'

'Yes,' I said. 'We have a problem – a sort of a mystery. Ah! Here's Cheapside, too. Good! We'll be glad to have his opinion as well.'

31

THE DOG DETECTIVE

THEN from beginning to end, leaving out nothing that I thought might be helpful, I told Kling the story of our midnight summons to the fire at Moorsden Manor and all that followed it.

Jip was right when he said that anyone might at first sight think that Kling was stupid. While I talked he went on chewing his boot as though his whole attention was absorbed in that and not in what I was saying. But I soon found out that he had not only heard what I had said, but that he remembered it, every word.

'Well,' he began when I was done, 'in a case like this the first thing I would do is to build up a story. By that I mean you lay the mystery out – you solve it before you begin, by guesswork, in other words. Then you go to work and see if you are right or not. Tell me : when you finally found Mr Throgmorton – or, rather, when he found you – had he anything with him ?'

'Yes,' I said, 'some small leather boxes.'

'Did you by any chance find out what they contained ?'

'Yes,' I said again. 'Matthew opened one when Throgmorton wasn't looking. It had four large diamond studs in it.'

Kling nodded thoughtfully.

'And these two ferocious watch-dogs,' he went on presently, 'weren't they usually kept *in*side the house ? Perhaps Matthew knows.'

I questioned the Cats'-meat-Man.

'Yes,' said he. 'And that's still another queer thing I hadn't thought of before. The dogs were always brought into the house after dark and left loose to roam where they would. When they killed that burglar, they caught him just as he was opening the silver drawer in the butler's pantry. I heard that from one of the gardeners. Yes, it was queer that that night Dina and Wolf were not inside the house at all. They were being kept by someone. It seemed as though they came from the stable.'

I interpreted to Kling. And he nodded again as though it all fitted in with his picture.

'Well, then,' he said, after a moment's thought, 'let us begin and build. Perhaps for the benefit of Matthew you had better explain to him once in a while what I am saying, so we can see whether he agrees with it or not. We will start off by supposing that since Mr Throgmorton was so annoyed with you – you who came to put the fire out – *that he lighted it himself.*'

I jumped slightly. It was such a startling idea.

'Just a minute, Kling,' I said. 'I'll put that to Matthew.'

The Cats'-meat-Man, when I told him, also jumped.

'Why, that's a notion!' said he. 'A notion and a half, by Jiminy! And yet it fits in with some things, all right. I'd been thinking all the time that he was trying to get us off the place because he was doing something up there he hadn't ougher. I never thought of his setting fire to his own mansion – must be worth thousands and thousands of pounds, that place, with all the stuff in it. And then he kicked because we'd broken the windows. That don't sound as though he didn't care about the house. ... Just the same, it's an idea worth followin' up. Tell the dog to go on.'

'You see,' Kling continued, 'the fact that Sidney Throgmorton had his jewellery with him, also that this was the only night that the dogs were not kept in the house, makes it look as though he expected the fire.'

'Yes,' I said, 'that's so. But his loss would have been enormous just the same.'

'Wait,' said Kling. 'Maybe we'll find that his loss would have been still more enormous if he didn't have the fire. ... Well, to proceed: Now, having supposed that Throgmorton set fire to his own house – it has been done before – I've known cases myself – the next question is: What did he want to burn it down for? He wanted to get rid of something, we'll say. What did he want to get rid of? Had he any people in it he wanted to kill?'

I questioned Matthew. The answer was: None that he knew of.

'Any brothers or sisters?' asked Kling.

'None,' said Matthew. 'That I know for sure.'

'Very well,' Kling went on, 'then he wanted to destroy some *thing*, since people are out of the question. Why didn't he find the thing and get rid of it, instead of burning down a valuable house? Because he had tried and couldn't find it? Possibly. And almost certainly, if it was –'

'A will?' I broke in.

'Exactly,' said Kling, nodding. 'Yet why destroy a will? Because in it he knew, or guessed, that his father had left the property, not to him, the son, but to some other parties. If there was no will he would get all the property because he was the only child. So, guessing there had been a will made; almost certain it was in that house; unable to find it himself, but terrified that someone else might – don't forget that he got rid of all the old servants and bought two ferocious watch-dogs to keep people out – finally he determines to burn the whole place up and the will with it. What does that loss matter when he had a dozen other houses and estates – which he never visited, fearing to leave the Manor lest someone find the will while he is gone!'

32

OLD MR THROGMORTON

'It fits, it fits!' cried Matthew, jumping up in his excitement when I had explained what Kling had said. 'The gardener told me the father and son could never get along together. And that's why Sidney Throgmorton stayed abroad most of the time till after the old man died. And the father didn't want it known that they couldn't agree, see? So of course he would keep the will dark. It all fits like a glove. The dog's a wizard. But listen: we ought to do something quickly. That man is liable to try and burn the house down again any minute.'

One would have thought, to hear the Cats'-meat-Man talk, that it was he who would lose most by the will's destruction. And I must confess that the fascination of the mystery and the desire to frustrate the iniquitous Sidney Throgmorton had me also in its grip by this time.

'Oh, I don't think he'll make another attempt in a hurry,' I said. 'It would look fishy. After all, he has got to be careful, you see. If he knows there was a will, then what he tried to do was a criminal offence – goodness, I don't wonder he was furious with us!'

'The next step for you, I should say,' Kling went on, 'is to try and find out to whom the old Throgmorton would have been most likely to leave his money.'

At that Cheapside, whom in our interest we had forgotten all about, hopped on to the table and started talking.

'Folks,' said he, 'I think I can help you there, maybe. I saw a good deal of the old Mr Throgmorton, and a mighty fine gentleman he was. It wasn't at Moorsden Manor that

I saw him, because he only spent a week or two out of every year here. But to one of his other places, Bencote Castle, down in Sussex, I used to go regular, at one time, in the early autumn. The old man, as perhaps you know, retired from business when he was getting on in years. And 'e spent 'is old age, pleasant like, raisin' prize stock, cows, sheep, and horses – specially heavy draught-horses. He was good to animals all round, was old Jonathan T. Throgmorton. He had bird-fountains put out in all his gardens, nesting-boxes in the trees and everything. And he gave one of his footmen the special job of throwing out crumbs every morning for the sparrows and wild birds. Some days, when the old man was well enough, he used to do it himself. That's how I came to know him. Besides all that, he did a whole lot towards making life easier for working animals – paid to have drinking-troughs put up for horses, and kept extra help-teams, at his own expense, on all the steep hills in more than one town where he had homes. He was a friend to animals and a fine old gent, if ever there was one. I shouldn't wonder, Tommy, if he left part of this fortune to the same cause, the happiness of animals.'

Before Cheapside had quite finished speaking I got out my pocket-book in which I had carefully preserved the scrap of parchment. I spread the fragment out and re-read the few words which had been nibbled from the will. They were in four lines. The first line ran : *trustees who shall have –* ' The second line, beginning a new paragraph, was : '*I bequeath –* ' The third : '*by said party or parties –*' And the last : '*an Association for pre –*'

To everyone's astonishment I suddenly sprang up and said :

'Let's all go and see the Doctor – just as quickly as we possibly can.'

The Manor mouse excused himself, saying that he ought to be getting back home as it was late and his wife might be anxious. As we left the room the white mouse told me he would accompany his friend as far as the gate and would rejoin me in a minute or two. Together the rest of us, Matthew, Jip, Kling, Cheapside and I, proceeded at once to the study, where we found John Dolittle, as usual, at work on his books.

'Doctor,' I cried, bursting in, 'I'm dreadfully sorry to interrupt you, but I really feel you ought to hear this.'

With a patient sigh he laid down his pen as I poured forth my tale.

'Now, don't you see, Doctor,' I ended, showing him the scrap of parchment again, 'it is practically certain that when this piece is joined to the rest that last line will read, 'an Association for the Prevention of Cruelty to Animals', or some such title. For that is the cause in which this man had already spent great sums of money while he was alive. And that is the cause which the wretched son Sidney Throgmorton has robbed of probably a large fortune. Doctor, it is the *animals* who have been cheated.'

We all watched the Doctor's face eagerly as he pondered for a silent moment over my somewhat dramatic harangue. At length I thought I saw from his expression signs of sympathy, if not agreement.

'But, Stubbins,' said he quietly, 'aren't you basing most of this on guesswork, conjecture – though I admit it sounds plausible enough. Tell me : what do you want me to do ?'

'Doctor,' I said, 'we've got to get that will.'

'Yes, yes, I quite see that,' said he. 'But how ? Even if we got into the house – risking arrest for burglary and all that – what chance would we stand of finding it, if Sidney Throgmorton, living there all the time and hunting for it ever since his father's death, couldn't find it ?'

I saw at once that he was right. The difficulties of the task I proposed were enormous. But while I stood there silent, discouraged and perplexed, I suddenly heard the white mouse out in the passage squeaking at the top of his voice:

'Tommy, Tommy! They've found it. They've found it! The mice have found the will!'

33

THE SECRET CUPBOARD

THE white mouse was so breathless with running when he appeared at the study door that he could hardly talk. I lifted him to the table, where between puffs he finally managed to give us his message.

Apparently, just as he was seeing the Manor mouse off at the gate, a rat had run up and said that they had at last located the document. The old man had hidden it, it seemed, in a secret cupboard on the top floor of the house. They couldn't get the will out because it was a large heavy roll of parchment; and the hole which they had made into the cupboard (through the brickwork at the back) was very, very small. Indeed, it was so tiny that the two rats who had made it couldn't get through it. But they could see that there were papers of some sort inside. So they had got the very smallest mouse in the Manor and sent him in to make an examination and give them a report. And they were now quite certain that the document was the will, because it was made of the same kind of parchment and had a corner missing corresponding to the one in my possession.

Well, as you can imagine, the excitement among us was

tremendous. And when, a moment later, the rat in question himself appeared, confirmed the story, and offered to lead the Doctor at once to the secret cupboard, I could see that the thrill of the Moorsden Manor Mystery was beginning at last to take hold of John Dolittle himself. Matthew was all for starting right away.

'No, now wait a minute,' said the Doctor. 'Not so fast. This is a serious thing. If we should be wrong and get caught we will have hard work to explain our actions – especially with Sidney Throgmorton anxious to put us all in jail, anyway. We must proceed carefully and make as few mistakes as possible. Let me see: what time is it? Eleven forty-five. We couldn't attempt it before two o'clock in the morning, anyhow. We must be sure everyone's abed first. Listen, Jip: you run over there to the Manor and tell – by the way, could you get into the grounds, do you think?'

'Oh, yes,' said Jip. 'I can slip through the bars of that big gate easily.'

'Well,' said the Doctor, 'don't be seen, for Heaven's sake. They might shoot you. Then just nose quietly round the house till you get a chance to speak to those two watchdogs, Dina and Wolf. Tell them to expect me about two o'clock. Goodness knows how I'm going to get into the house. That I'll have to find out when I get there. Anyway, tell them not to be worried or give any alarm if they hear latches being forced or anything like that. Do you understand?'

'All right,' said Jip. And he hopped through the open window into the darkness of the garden and was gone.

'Now, the next thing,' said the Doctor, 'we'll need a rope. See if you can find my alpine rope up in the attic, Stubbins, will you, please?'

'Shall we be taking Bumpo along, Doctor?' asked

Matthew. 'Better, don't you think? He's a handy man in a tight place.'

'Er – yes, I suppose so,' said John Dolittle. 'Though the trouble with Bumpo is that he is sometimes a trifle too handy.'

'Then I'll go and start getting him woke up,' said the Cats'-meat-Man. 'It's a long job as a rule.'

Well, although we had two and a quarter hours in which to make our preparations it did not seem any too long. One after another the Doctor, Matthew, Kling, Cheapside, and the white mouse and I would keep thinking of things we ought to take, or do, to ensure success to the expedition. And when John Dolittle finally looked at his watch and said that we ought to be starting, it did not seem as though more than a few minutes had elapsed since he had made up his mind to embark upon the venture.

Fortunately there would be no moon till somewhere about three o'clock in the morning. So, to begin with anyhow, we had the protection of pretty complete darkness.

In spite of the fact that I shared Polynesia's confidence in the Doctor's luck and success, I must confess I felt quite thrilled by the risks ahead of us as we quietly opened the gate and trailed down to the road.

The Doctor and Matthew had worked out most of the details of our campaign before we left and had assigned to each of us what parts we were to play. So there was no talking as we plodded silently along the road towards the Manor.

At a point where the limb of a large ash tree overhung the high wall of the estate we halted and the Doctor uncoiled his rope. With the aid of a stone tied to a long length of twine, we got the rope's end hauled up over the branch and down to the road again. Up this we all swarmed in turn. Meanwhile Cheapside kept watch in the branches above to see that no one surprised us on the Manor side, and Kling below kept an eye open for late wayfarers that might pass along the road.

When all of us were inside the grounds and the rope hauled over after us, Kling went off to enter, like Jip, through the bars of the gate.

When I got down out of the tree the first thing I noticed was Jip's white shadow flitting across the sward to meet us.

'It's all right,' he whispered to the Doctor. 'I've told Dina and Wolf. They say they will be on the look out for you and will show you round the place when you get in.'

'Yes, but it is the getting in that is going to be the job, I'm afraid,' muttered John Dolittle. 'Listen, Jip: from here I've no idea of even where the house lies – through all this shrubbery and park-land. Lead us to it, will you? And bring us up on the wooded side. We don't want to cross any open spaces.'

'Very good,' said Jip. 'I'll take you to the kitchen-garden side. You'll have cover all the way up. But if you should get spotted and have to run for it, tell everyone to follow me. I know the easiest and shortest way out.'

Then in single file we trailed after Jip, who kept us behind bushes and hedges for what seemed like a good ten minutes' walk. Suddenly we found ourselves against the wall of the house itself. Here I noticed for the first time that Kling had rejoined us.

'Listen,' I heard him whisper to the Doctor, 'you've got that rat in your pocket still, haven't you? – the one who lives here.'

'Yes,' said John Dolittle. 'And the white mouse, too.'

'Well, that rat is your best chance for getting in,' said Kling. 'If you let Matthew force a lock you're liable to have complications with the police afterwards. Send the rat into the house through a hole – he'll know lots of them leading down into the cellar. And tell him to get you the master's latchkey. It'll be in his bedroom, on the dressing-table, you may be sure.'

'Splendid!' whispered the Doctor. And he at once took the rat from his pocket and explained to him what Kling had said. Then he let him go upon the ground and we waited.

It was about five minutes later, I should say, when I felt something small and sharp hit me on the head. Even through my cap it stung. From my head it bounced to the ground. And by the dim starlight I could see it shining dully where it lay. I picked it up. It was a small key. Apparently the master's bedroom window was directly above our heads; and the rat, to save time, had thrown the key out to us.

I slipped it into the Doctor's hand and in silence we moved round towards the front of the house.

34

THE WILD RIDE OF THE WHITE MOUSE

IT had been agreed that only Matthew should accompany the Doctor to the top floor. I was to remain downstairs in the hall; and Bumpo was to stay outside the house. His and my parts in the plot were mostly those of watching and standing on guard. In case of emergency we had signals arranged and were to assemble at a certain point.

As the Doctor very, very quietly opened the front door with the latchkey I got my first real scare of the evening. With uncanny suddenness, both together, the two great ferocious heads of the watch-dogs popped out to greet him.

Within the hall where the darkness was quite intense, I confess that I was quite glad that my duties carried me no farther. As we had arranged, I sat down on the floor by the front door and began my watch. Jip, thank goodness, stayed with me. Matthew and the Doctor, each with a hand on the collar of one of the guiding watch-dogs, were led away swiftly and silently through the inky blackness, up the carpeted stairs, to the rooms above.

It seemed a perfect eternity that they were gone. Before the evening was over I decided that I didn't care for the profession of burglary a bit. It was a little too thrilling. Every time the breeze rattled a window or swung a curtain whispering across the floor, I was certain that we had been discovered and someone was coming after us with a pistol or a club. It was a great temptation to open the front door and let in the little light of the starry sky without. But I had been told to keep it closed lest the draught be detected by any of the household.

At last Jip whispered:

'Don't get scared now if someone bumps into you. They're coming down the stairs again. I can smell 'em.'

A moment later the wet muzzle of Dina, leading the Doctor across the hall, dabbed me in the ear. It was a good thing Jip had warned me – I should probably have started hitting out in all directions if he hadn't. I rose and carefully swung open the front door. The dim forms of the Doctor and Matthew passed out. I followed. With a pat of thanks John Dolittle turned and shut the two dogs in behind us, letting the tongue of the night-latch gently into its socket with the key. Then he took the rat from his pocket, gave him the key and set him on the ground. From somewhere out of the general gloom of the garden Bumpo's huge figure emerged and joined us.

Once more under Jip's guidance we began the journey across the park towards the walls. I was simply burning up to ask the Doctor if he had succeeded, but I managed to restrain my curiosity till we stood again beneath the ash tree. Then at last I felt it was safe to whisper:

'Did you get it?'

'Yes,' he said. 'It's in my pocket. Everything went all right. We were able to open the cupboard and close it again too, leaving it so no one would know we were there. But, of course, I haven't had a chance to read the will yet. Come along now, where's that rope?'

Again, one by one, we swarmed to the top of the wall, transferred the dangling rope to the other side and slid quietly down into the roadway.

With a general sigh we set off towards home. As we passed the gate we noticed the grey of the dawn showing in the east. Like silent ghosts Kling and Jip slipped out through the bars and dropped in behind the procession.

On reaching the house we all hurried to the study. I got some candles lighted while the Doctor spread the will out on the table. It was a tense moment for all of us as we leant over his shoulder.

Sure enough, a piece had been bitten out of the document at the corner. And when I added the fragment I had in my pocket it fitted perfectly. Then, without going through the preliminary preamble of the document, the Doctor traced that paragraph with his finger. This is what he read out: 'I bequeath the sum of One Hundred Thousand Pounds for the endowment of an Association for the Prevention of Cruelty to Animals. The Trustees will select –'

But he was not permitted to get any farther. Matthew, Bumpo and I suddenly started cheering and dancing round the table. And it was quite some minutes before our enthusiasm had let off enough steam to allow us to listen to any more.

As we settled down into our chairs again I noticed the Doctor staring fixedly at something Matthew was turning over in his fingers. I started as I saw what it was – one of the diamond shirt-studs from Sidney Throgmorton's little leather box.

'Er – where – did you get that, Matthew?' asked the Doctor, in a low, somewhat fearful voice.

'Oh, this?' said the Cats'-meat-Man, trying hard not to look guilty. 'This is a little souvenir I brought along from the Manor.'

For a moment the Doctor seemed too horrified to speak.

'Well,' Matthew went on, 'it wasn't his, you know, after all, with him robbin' the animals of that whole fortune what was coming to them accordin' to the will.'

But when, how, did you take it, Matthew?' asked the Doctor. 'I thought you were with me all the time.'

'Oh, I just dropped into his bedroom to take a look around, as we passed his door going up the stairs,' said Matthew. 'These pretty playthings was in a box on the dressin'-table, and I couldn't resist the temptation of bringin' one along as a souvenir.'

With his hand to his head the Doctor sank into a chair as if stunned.

'Oh, Matthew, Matthew!' he murmured. 'I thought you had promised me to give up that – that sort of thing for good.'

For a moment we were all silent. Finally the Doctor said:

'Well, I don't know what we are to do now, really I don't.'

The white mouse crawled up my sleeve from the table and whispered in my ear:

'What's the matter with the Doctor? What has happened?'

I explained to him as quickly and as briefly as I could.

'Give me that stud, Doctor,' said he, suddenly darting across the table to John Dolittle. 'I'll get it back into its box before you can say Jack Robinson.'

'Goodness! Do you think you could?' cried the Doctor. Immediately all cheered up. 'Oh, but look: the daylight is here now. The disappearance of the diamond is most likely already discovered. And think of the time it would take you to travel there – at your pace!'

'Doctor, it wouldn't take long if he rode on my back,' Jip put in. 'If I carry him as far as the house he can soon pop in through a hole and slip upstairs. It's worth trying.'

'All right,' said the Doctor. 'Any port in a storm.'

And to Matthew's great disappointment he leant across the table, took the valuable jewel out of his hands and gave it to the white mouse.

'You'll save us from a terrible mess,' he said, 'if you can get it there in time. Good luck to you!'

The white mouse took the stud in his paws, jumped on to Jip's back and disappeared through the garden window at a gallop.

After he had gone there was an embarrassed, uncomfortable pause. Finally the Doctor said:

'Er – Stubbins and Bumpo: you will not of course – supposing that this matter ends satisfactorily – mention it, ever, to a living soul.'

Ill at ease, but very much in earnest, we nodded our promise of silence.

'As for you, Matthew,' the Doctor went on, 'I must warn you now, once and for all, that if any other occurrence of er – this sort takes place we shall have to sever relations permanently. I know I can trust you where my own property is concerned, but I must feel secure that you will regard the property of others in the same way. If not, we can have nothing further to do with one another. Do you understand?'

'Yes, I understand, Doctor,' said Matthew in a low voice. 'I ought to have known I might be putting you in an awkward situation. But – well, no more need be said.'

The Doctor turned as though to go into the garden. He looked about him for his hat. And suddenly a look of horror came slowly into his face.

'Stubbins!' he gasped. 'Where is it?'

'Don't tell me,' I cried, 'that you left it again – *in the Manor!*'

35

OUR ARREST

IT was true. In the thrill and excitement of our nocturnal adventure none of us had noticed whether the Doctor had come away from the Manor bareheaded or with his hat on. But now that we came to think of it we could all recall that he had worn it on the way there. Next, he himself remembered clearly that in getting into the secret cupboard he had laid it aside on a chair because it was in the way.

'Dear me!' he sighed, shaking his head. 'That's the kind of a burglar *I* am – leave my hat behind me, the one thing that everybody in the neighbourhood would recognize as mine .... Hah! It would be funny if it wasn't so serious. Well, more than ever depends on the white mouse now. Dear, dear! Anyhow,' he added as Dab-Dab appeared at the door, 'let's not meet our troubles half-way. Breakfast ready, Dab-Dab?'

'No,' said the housekeeper, coming forward into the room and lowering her voice. 'But there are three men walking up the garden path. One is carrying your hat. And one is a policeman.'

At that Matthew sprang up and in a twinkling was half out of the garden window. Then, apparently changing his mind, he stopped.

'No, Doctor,' said he, coming back into the room, 'I ain't goin' to skedaddle and leave you to face the music. I've bin in jail before. I'll tell 'em I've done it.'

'Look here, Matthew,' said John Dolittle firmly: 'I want you to do one thing only throughout the rest of this business, and that is to keep your mouth closed tight – unless I ask you to talk. Stubbins, will you please let them in?'

I went and opened the door. I knew all three men by sight. One was Sidney Throgmorton; the other his lodge-keeper; and the third our local Police Sergeant. The Sergeant's manner was distinctly apologetic. He knew John Dolittle, and this duty was distasteful to him. Throgmorton's behaviour, on the other hand, was offensive from the start. He brushed by me before I had invited him to come in and walked straight to the Doctor's study.

'Ah!' he cried. 'We have the whole lot here, Sergeant – the same party exactly that came pretending to put the fire out when they wanted to learn their way around the house they meant later to rob. Put them all under arrest and bring them at once to the Manor.'

The Sergeant, while he was somewhat impressed by Throgmorton's position in the community, knew what his duties were without being told. He addressed himself to John Dolittle.

'This gentleman has brought a charge, Doctor,' he said. 'A valuable diamond was stolen from his house last night and your hat was found on the premises this morning. I shall have to ask you to come up to the Manor, please.'

We were all glad that the early hour gave us practically empty streets to walk through. For certainly our party with the Sergeant for escort would have set gossip running all over Puddleby if there had been many abroad to see us.

Hardly a word was said the whole way by anyone except Throgmorton, to whose indignant fumings no one seemed to want to make any reply.

At the house the old man-servant let us in and we went straight upstairs to the master's bedroom. Here Throgmorton at once plunged into a dramatic recital, for the Sergeant's benefit, of how he had arisen at his usual hour of six and had at once noticed that his stud-box had been moved from the place where he had left it the night before. He opened it, he said, and found one stud missing. After the servants had been summoned and a search made of the house, the Doctor's hat had been found in a room on the top floor. This, and the fact that we had all behaved in a suspicious manner the night of the fire, at once convicted us in his mind as the culprits.

'Just a minute,' said the Doctor. 'Is the box now in the exact place where you found it when you got up?'

'Yes,' said Throgmorton.

'Well, would you show us, please, just how you went to the dressing-table and opened it?'

'Certainly,' said Throgmorton. 'I walked from the bed, like this, and first threw back the curtains of the window, so. Then one glance at the dressing-table told me something was wrong. I stepped up to it – so – lifted the box and opened it. Like this. . . . What the –'

At that last exclamation of astonishment we all four breathed a secret sigh of relief. For it told us that the white mouse had done his work. I shall never forget Throgmorton's face as he stood there, staring into the box he had taken up to demonstrate with. In it there were not three studs, as he had expected, but the complete set of four.

The Sergeant looked over his shoulder.

'There's been some mistake, sir, hasn't there?' said he quietly.

'There's b-b-b-been some trickery,' cried Throgmorton, spluttering. Indeed his discomfited indignation was understandable enough in the circumstances. He would much sooner have got John Dolittle into jail than have recovered his stud. And this small quiet man seemed to have a knack for making a fool of him at the most dramatic moments.

'If you didn't do it,' he snarled, swinging round on the Doctor and pointing a fat accusing finger at him, 'how did your hat come to be in my house?'

'I think,' said the Doctor, 'it would be best if I gave you an answer to that question in private.'

'No,' snapped Throgmorton. 'If it's the truth there's no harm in the Police Sergeant hearing it.'

'As you wish,' said the Doctor. 'But I thought you would prefer it that way. It has to do with a will whose existence we discovered by accident.'

Astonishment, fear, hatred flitted across Throgmorton's face in quick succession during the short moment that passed before he answered.

'All right,' he said sullenly at last. 'We will go down to the library.'

In a silent, very thoughtful procession we returned down the several flights of stairs. At the tail of it came Matthew and myself.

'Thank goodness for the white mouse, Tommy!' he whispered in my ear. 'But I don't like trusting that fellow alone with the Doctor.'

'Don't worry,' I answered. 'We'll be outside the door.

He'll hardly dare to start any violence with the Sergeant here as a witness. His game's up.'

I heard the big grandfather clock in the hall strike as the Doctor and Throgmorton went into the library and closed the door behind them. And it was exactly three-quarters of an hour before they came out.

Throgmorton was very white, but quite quiet. He immediately addressed himself to the policeman.

'The charge is withdrawn, Sergeant,' he said. 'A mistake – for which I tender my apologies to – er – all concerned. I'm sorry I got you up here so early when there was no need.'

Again in silence we trailed across the wide carpeted hall and out into the gravel court.

At the gate we bade farewell to the Sergeant, whose direction was a different one from ours. I noticed that the Doctor made no comment upon the matter to him.

When he was well out of earshot Matthew asked eagerly:

'But, Doctor, how did you explain your hat's being there?'

'I didn't,' said John Dolittle. 'But I told him that all four of us were convinced he lit that fire himself. And after that he was much more anxious that I should keep my mouth shut than that I should do any explaining. He has got rather scared of me now, I imagine. And he probably thinks that I can prove he lit the fire. Which I can't. But it is just as well that he should think so, because I feel sure he did. He is going back to Australia now.'

'To Australia!' cried Matthew. 'Why?'

'Well, he has to earn a living, you see,' said the Doctor. 'The will left not only the hundred thousand pounds for the prevention of cruelty to animals, but when I came to read it through I found that it left the rest to other charities.'

When the outcome of the Moorsden Manor mystery became generally known in the Dolittle Zoo, jubilation and rejoicing broke forth and lasted two whole days. Accustomed as it was to celebration, Animal Town admitted it had never seen the like before. The white mouse's genius for parade organization surpassed itself; and he was elected to a second term of office as mayor on the strength of it.

He felt that since animals in general had by the Doctor's victory come into such a considerable fortune, this occasion should be made a larger and more important one than any in the history of the zoo. So for the second day's celebrations he got the Doctor's permission to send out an invitation to all the creatures of the neighbourhood who wished to come. An enormous amount of preparation was made in expectation of a large attendance. The whole zoo was most gaily decorated, with ribbons and bunting by day and with lanterns and fireworks by night. Great quantities of all sorts of things to eat and drink were bought and set out at several buffets in the enclosure.

But the crowd that actually did come was even much, much vaster than had been anticipated. All the regular members of the Rat and Mouse Club, the Rabbits' Apartment House, the Home for Cross-bred Dogs, the Badgers' Tavern, the Squirrels' Hotel and the Foxes' Meeting House had to set to and do duty as hosts. So did Gub-Gub, the pushmipullyu, Chee-Chee, Too-Too, Dab-Dab, and Polynesia. And even with this extra help it was only by working like bees that they managed to feed and entertain that enormous crowd of visitors.

As for the Doctor, Matthew, Bumpo and me, we were kept busy running between the house and the town for more, and still more, refreshments, as the ever-increasing attendance did away with what we had already. Too-Too, the accountant, told me afterwards that according to his books we had bought more than a wagon-load of lettuce, three hundredweight of corn and birdseed, close on a ton of bones and meat, four large cheeses and two dozen loaves – besides a great number of delicacies in smaller quantity.

Within the old bowling-green it was almost impossible to move along the lawns, so thronged were they with hedge-hogs, moles, squirrels, stoats, rats, badgers, mice, voles, otters, hares, and what not. At frequent intervals cheers for the Doctor, old Mr Throgmorton, or his Association for the Prevention of Cruelty to Animals, would break out in some corner and be rapidly taken up all over the vast assembly. Every tree and shrub in the zoo enclosure – and throughout the whole of the Doctor's garden, too – was just packed and laden with perching birds of all kinds and sizes, from wrens to herons. The din of their chatter was constant and terrific.

Before the day was over the grass of the bowling-green was all worn away by the continuous passing of those millions of feet. And after the guests had departed it took the members of the Dolittle Zoo another whole day to clear away the scraps and put the place in order.

ABOUT THE AUTHOR

Hugh Lofting was of English-Irish parentage. He was born on January 14, 1886, at Maidenhead, England, and as a young man chose the profession of civil engineering as a means to travel and adventure. Before the War he built railways in West Africa and Canada but it was in the trenches of France that he first began writing for children. The first Doctor Dolittle stories were illustrated letters written to his own children during the War. When the family went to America in 1919, the children were induced to show their precious manuscripts to a publisher and *The Story of Doctor Dolittle* was published in 1920. After that Mr. Lofting was forced to give up his entire time to writing and illustrating his increasingly popular books for young people and the famous Doctor Dolittle series grew up.

All the Lofting books are illustrated by the author and are enjoyed by children of all ages.

Hugh Lofting died 27th September, 1947.